HEAVEN'S EDGE

HEAVEN'S EDGE

ROMESH GUNESEKERA

GROVE PRESS
New York

First published in Great Britain in 2002 by
Bloomsbury Publishing Plc, London, England

Published simultaneously in Canada
Printed in the United States of America

FIRST AMERICAN EDITION

Library of Congress Cataloging-in-Publication Data
Gunesekera, Romesh.
  Heaven's edge / Romesh Gunesekera.
    p. cm.
  ISBN 0-8021-1735-X
  1. Women environmentalists — Fiction. 2. Political violence —
  Fiction. 3. Kidnapping victims — Fiction. 4. Women
  farmers — Fiction. 5. Islands — Fiction. I. Title.

PR9440.9.G86 H43 2003
823'.914 — dc21   2002035335

Grove Press
841 Broadway
New York, NY 10003

03 04 05 06 07   10 9 8 7 6 5 4 3 2 1

ACKNOWLEDGEMENTS

My thanks to Alexandra Pringle. Also to Marian McCarthy, Chiki Sarkar, and all the others at Bloomsbury; Bill Hamilton and Sara Fisher at A M Heath; Frances Coady.

I would also like to thank the many people who have shared with me their expertise, their gardens or their houses as I wrote. I am grateful, in particular, to those who offered me the experiences of their pasts, near and far.

Finally, special thanks to Tanisa and Shanthi for music and inspiration, and Helen without whom this book, too, could not be.

Helen

Kill not the Moth nor Butterfly . . .
William Blake

CONTENTS

I

NUBURN

I ARRIVED on this island, by boat, the night of the fullest moon I had ever seen in my life. The sky was clear and the sea phosphorescent; the coastline, from a distance, looked entrancing. Two flying fish, accidentally netted, were released by the boatman as we docked at the pier of the Palm Beach Hotel. I thought that was auspicious.

The steps down from the jetty were a little rickety and the iron handrail had corroded in several places, but the ground was firm. I stood on the beach and breathed in. I felt elated: this was the moment I had been waiting for. Even the breeze was warm.

I followed a footpath littered with dead urchins and broken crabclaws and climbed up to the hotel overlooking the bay. The gate at the top wouldn't fully open and I had to squeeze past a giant screw-pine; one of its thorny leaves scraped the sea that had coated my arm. In front of me a blue plumbago shrub exposed a few pale flakes broken off the moon. A yellow light on the garden terrace blinked and went out. I crossed the strip of lawn not knowing quite what to expect.

The Palm Beach Hotel, I had been warned, was thirty kilometres from Maravil and the only other hotel open to visitors; it had no brochure and no guaranteed amenities.

When I reached the long, low building I could see that the paint on the outside wall had cracked and peeled; a trail of blisters ran down one side of the portico and the wooden beams of the veranda were warped. The hotel sign had not been repaired.

I brushed the sand from my shoes and pushed open the door, careful not to touch the loose glass in the frame. I rolled my case into the foyer feeling a little nervous. The floor was made out of coarse, uneven granite and the small plastic wheels fixed to the bag rattled over the bumps; there was no other sound. In a corner, behind a desk, I noticed a receptionist asleep. His narrow face had crumbled at the edges; his tunic was unbuttoned. I waited at least a minute before gently rapping on the counter.

'I have a reservation,' I said in slow English.

The cowls over his eyes slid open. He stared at me.

'From the Sea-Link Corporation,' I added, trying to be a little upbeat. I had a fortnight confirmed with an option to renew, indefinitely if I wanted to. I had been told there was very little business these days anywhere on the island.

Opening a large ledger, the receptionist flicked a page over. 'No,' he grunted. The lids slipped down again, leaving only a pair of narrow slits through which he watched me. 'We have no reservation.'

I started to panic and fumbled around for my papers.

'You want a room?' he asked then, as if issuing a challenge.

'Yes.' I found my passport and the booking docket. I offered them to him.

He riffled through the documents. After some time he relented. 'Maybe one, but no discount.'

4

He pushed the passport back to me, together with a registration card and a faded tariff sheet. While I filled in the card, he inched out from behind the desk. He was a small, scrawny man and seemed to have some trouble with his foot. He limped down a dim corridor. I quickly signed the card and followed him.

The room he led me to was the last in the line. He switched on the light; it barely made a difference but I felt relieved. The bed was large – king-sized – and solid; inviting despite the mangy blue coverlet. He pointed at the shrouded windows. 'Sea view.'

A gecko emerged from behind the frosted lampshade fixed to the wall.

'Good,' I nodded. The boat I had travelled on would have left by now. It wasn't due back again until the end of the month. 'I'll take the room,' I said, 'at least until the next boat.'

He made an odd guttural sound and then stared at my bag with his head awkwardly lowered. It took me a while to realise he was waiting for a tip. I handed him a ten-dollar note. The foreign exchange made him, briefly, almost garrulous.

'Pool, minibar.' He jerked his thumb and pivoted, cracking his joints. 'Breakfast not included. Extra charge.'

'OK,' I said. That was not what I had come for. I had not wanted to cruise in on a cut-price package deal, full-board or half. I was on a mission to explore an older terrain and discover for myself what was best to remember, and what might be better to forget, here and in my life. I would have told him so, but he looked much too sullen and worn-out to care.

After he left, I drew back the curtains and opened the windows to let the sea breeze in. There was no air-conditioner.

It suited me; I wanted to know what a night in a hot country was really like. To hear the crickets and the cicadas, to smell the citrus and the citronella, the warm earth dreaming, and feel the spirit of the place brush against my skin.

My grandfather Eldon had warned me, as I was growing up between the fig trees and rat-runs of a rowdy, congested London, 'You must decide for yourself how you should live in this world. Like a flower seeking light, we each go where we find our best sustenance. Yet in reaching out – free as we are – we have to be careful not to lose more than can ever be gained.' He would lecture me in his sheltered garden, pruning his roses, watering his delphiniums, trying to pass to me the lessons of what he called his extended innings, while I trained my ears to the roar of aircraft coming in to land, one after another, at nearby Heathrow. He was gravest when he spoke about my father's undertakings. 'We have a choice, you know, and sometimes that is hard. Sometimes we have to choose between people and places, the sky and the earth. War and peace.' He lifted his large, wavering hands as though he wanted to admonish my dad – his absent son Lee, the ace air warrior – through me, and I watched as though Eldon was my absent father: each of us occupying the other's empty space.

Both my father and my grandfather had been quick to escape their formative traps. Eldon by coming to England from this apparent pearl of an island, and Lee, fifty years later, by leaving England, his birthplace. I never had the same compulsion to move – until the day my father's voice returned and urged me out.

★   ★   ★

6

In the morning, I woke up hot and hungry. The glare from the window flattened the room. I wondered what the rest of the place looked like in daylight. I changed into my shorts and went in search of breakfast.

A couple of parasols had been put out on the terrace and two waiters were squatting down by the pool. I ordered the local menu and was served a plate of raw roti, some red desiccated coconut and a glass of sour undrinkable juice. I asked for bottled water and was given a jug. It was probably permanent hunger, or some parasite in the gut, that made the staff seem so unfriendly, but I didn't think of it then. I just felt disappointed.

Most of that first day I spent adjusting to the heat and the humidity. It was something I had only ever experienced before in horticultural glasshouses, and it was difficult for me to believe that the temperature was not temporary.

Inside the hotel I walked around in a daze, ducking into the dingy comfort of the arcade room every half hour or so to punch a bunch of pinball buttons and swill another glass of iced lotus-brew. The atmosphere, even in the aromatherapy room, was absolutely stultifying. Nowhere did I see any sign of other guests. It didn't surprise me, given the warnings about civil strife, oppression and levels of residual radiation; quite apart, that is, from the service.

Late in the afternoon I dipped into the shady saline pool to cool down and recover the plans I had hatched on the boat, or even earlier, while I was still wired to my home-web, looking for news of this forgotten, assaulted island; or listening to my father's last recorded words.

When I got out of the water, I heard the buzz of a small aircraft and saw a military plane disappear behind the ailing cassias. Although there were no obvious transport facilities at the hotel, I was still confident I could find a way to visit some of the places Lee and Eldon had been to on their one and only journey abroad together. The journey that had changed my father's life.

He was seventeen when he first came here, brought to pay his respects to the ancestral land Eldon himself had spurned for decades. They had visited graveyards and sleepy suburbs; they had done a grand tour of the country which Eldon recounted time and again over the years. 'We went everywhere: the wildlife reserves, the ancient cities – more ruined now than ever before – up to the cool tea-hills, and then down through miles and bloody miles of those damn low-country coconut plantations.' I still remember how Eldon would pause and then mock me with his calypso version of my juvenile dub, 'Whole generations went to pot, you know, chasing the golden bloody coconut . . .' But, despite ridiculing the coconut kings of those days, his fondest recollection of that trip was the hunt for an ancestral home in his so-called low-country: a farm cottage in a twenty-acre coconut estate where he spent his holidays. He would conjure up the house for me. 'It had a thatched roof, and whitewashed walls. A sand garden with lantana shrubs and bougainvillaea. Hundreds of butterflies. And a breadfruit tree. I loved that place, my little Eden, so much more than the big manor house that our lot liked to pretend was the family heritage.' Sometimes he would bring out his crinkled maps and show me the web of journeys that held him and his son together, like a memory of paradise, after their return. His brown finger would trace their route along a network of red roads as though he was trying to soothe the veins of a lachrymose eye. 'We looked all over for that little house I had loved, but it had disappeared. The shape of the land itself had changed. Political gerrymandering had played socks with every bloody thing. I couldn't find my way. But looking for it, you know, was almost good enough . . .' He never returned to the island.

My father, on the other hand, seemed to have seen something that the older man could not. Something irresistible that brought him back, again and again. First to meet my mother, on her first long-haul holiday; and then again for their honeymoon; finally it brought him back in the middle of a war, for ever.

On my second morning I got up earlier, before the heat became unbearable, and took a walk outside the walls of the hotel. A broad strip of macadam meandered up to a sentry-point. I noticed the flash of mirror-light as a gun, or camera lens, hidden in the pill-box caught the rays of the sun. Although there were no soldiers to be seen, I didn't go any closer.

In the other direction, about five hundred metres down the road, was the village. I was keen to explore it, imagining that perhaps there I might discover the hidden charm of a long-suffering but colourful land.

I found a few ramshackle bungalows and, within the ramparts of an old fort, a pockmarked shopping mart boasting a drug store and a couple of bazaar stalls with some trinkets and a few essential dry goods like rice, flour and soap. Hardly any people were around. Inside a bakery, I spotted a couple of women in muted saris and a solitary man in a sarong, his shoulders drooped as though the blades had been ripped off. I tried to talk to them – English was supposed to have become the common link language along the coast – but no one was willing to speak to me. The women quickly retreated, and the man simply stared at me as if he had been hypnotised. The sense of subjugation was something I had not expected on an island so infused with myth and mystery. This was a place, it seemed to me then, devoid of any joy past, present or future. It was impossible to imagine what the attraction could have been for anyone.

As the days passed, I began to feel disheartened. The sun seemed cancerous on my skin, and the water was starting to feel too hot for swimming, even in the dark. I thought, if only I could reach one of the famous sites Eldon had talked about I might gain some satisfaction but there seemed no way of getting anywhere. I didn't have any proper information on where I could travel; I didn't even have an up-to-date map, only historical charts. Nothing else had been available. The hotel staff, when they deigned to appear, were hopeless. The receptionist would always summon the bellboy whenever I asked about excursions. 'Try village, sir,' was the bellboy's refrain, and he would scratch his ear violently whenever I complained that nobody there even bothered to listen.

'What about the jeep?' I asked the boy one morning, having seen him drive it into a garage. 'Can't I hire it?'

'Not possible, sir. Special approval required.' He put the keys in his little brown box and banged down the lid.

Nobody was able to tell me who gave 'special approval'. Even the barman at the cocktail hut pruned his lips and withdrew into his shell when I tried to question him. Perhaps I should have learned one of the local languages before I came, but I don't think it would have helped. It seemed I was in a place where conformity, or silence, was the only safe strategy for survival, and ignorance a kind of haven.

I was so disgruntled I spent the rest of the day trashing the decrepit minibar in my room. This could not be the same island that Eldon had talked about, that my father had loved, that I had read so much about. I had seen no animals, no birds, hardly any life. The trees, the plants, the buildings, the land, everything was drab. That evening, when I emerged, I banged into the drinks trolley parked at the poolside and knocked over an ice bucket. I ordered more lotus-brew and a packet of mouldy buns and derided the barman. I was too sozzled to care what he thought of me.

I felt thoroughly ashamed the next day and wanted to apologise to him. I looked all over the hotel; I couldn't find him. There was nobody around to say sorry to.

I decided then it was time to pull myself together and do whatever I could on my own. Six days had passed since I had landed. There was no point in hanging around. I thought I'd go into the scrub, at least, and see what I could find there. Explore as far as I could by foot, if nothing else. It was midday. The heat was searing, but I felt it had to be now or never. Walking, at least, was not forbidden. Any restricted area, I reckoned, would be fenced off or something. The rules would become clear, if there was a danger of violation; that seemed to be the way programmes ran everywhere.

I headed for the outer ramparts of the village. A dusty dog, stretched out in the shade, roused itself briefly; there was no other sign of life. A hundred metres beyond the old walls and piles of rubble, I came to a path that led down to a small sandy cove. A simple stretch of sand, sea and sky with the remains of the old fort on one side and a small stream trickling down into the sea on the other.

The freshwater at the mouth of the stream seemed cooler than the sea by the hotel and I was tempted to stay there until the sun eased, but I didn't want to lose the momentum I had built up. I wanted to get further, while I could. Much as I liked the cove, I decided to leave it for another day.

Near the stream a much wider path – more of a cart track – continued, leading I assumed to the next village, perhaps one more hospitable. I walked along it for about an hour, passing on the way a small boarded-up factory and a waste pit. Then I came to a turnoff where the mud between the hard, sharp ridges was still soft.

I saw pug marks. Big ones. They were made by the paws of a large animal, maybe from one of Eldon's celebrated game parks. Anything was possible: that was the point, I told myself, about an island of dreams.

I followed the prints until the track itself dwindled to a thin groove barely visible in the long grass. Then the vegetation grew thicker and thornier. The path disappeared. Scrub turned to jungle, wildwood and dung bramble. I carried on, feeling a little apprehensive but also quite chuffed at having come close to a jungle habitat. I didn't mind missing the next village. Picking my way through a tangle of trees and bushes I reached the edge of a small pond, no bigger than a playground paddling pool; a layer of green and brown duckweed covered most of the surface. Near the crust a few blanched flowers soaked in the sun. Sharp, thin leaves hung motionless from the trees. It seemed a scene out of the ancient chronicles Eldon used to try to interest me in when I was young. The heat, even with the water close by, was intense; the skin on my top lip burned as I exhaled. I tried to remember what I had once learned about stilling the mind and cooling the body. I felt a little dizzy. Perhaps it was a premonition. I wiped the perspiration around my eyes and tried to contemplate life after death. Then I noticed a movement in the bushes on the other side of the pond. I held my breath, hardly daring to hope I might observe some real wildlife: a langur or a hoopoe, perhaps a loris, or even the leopard whose tracks I was convinced I had seen. I felt a thrill I had never felt before, the promise of a glimpse into the primeval, but what emerged instead was a young woman in a yellow T-shirt and patchwork jeans.

At the water's edge she crouched down over a small bamboo cage and quickly released a catch. The speed and sureness with which she moved in the heat was hard to believe. I stepped forward to see what she had with her, and snapped a twig by accident. She looked up startled. Hastily she shook the cage, poised to run.

'Wait.' I bared my hands to show I meant her no harm. It could have been merely animal instinct, but I felt drawn to her. I went over. She shook back her long black hair. Her face was brimming with light. I couldn't stop staring.

A pair of green doves peeked out of the open cage. 'Shoo!' Her fingers danced in the air and the birds flew up in a clumsy flurry of brilliant feathers. They took refuge in one of the trees behind her, dislodging a small red fruit.

She kept her eyes on me while she bent down to pick it up. Her arm was trembling, but she looked more annoyed than frightened at being found out. Her face tightened; she seemed to suck in the air around her. The breeze turned the leaves above her head and I heard the flapping of wings again. The birds cooed.

'Emerald doves?' I asked, for some absurd reason expecting the words to placate her. I recognised the birds and was glad that they conformed to the jewelled picture I had from my boyhood bird books. The way she held herself without moving reminded me of something in myself. It was not desire but a kind of energy that absorbed as much as it gave out. I took a step closer.

The nerves straining inside her loosened, freeing her face briefly from irritation into surprise. 'You know emerald doves?' She brushed her hair back from her eyes, knotting it and pulling at the strands. Her nails were short but shaped and shiny; a thin metal bracelet slipped down one wrist. Streaks of sweat marked her face making her look flustered. The puffs under her eyes were wet and thin rings glistened around her slightly swollen neck. A few drops trickled to the seam of her top creating a small damp pattern in the cloth.

'You speak English?'

She nodded, perplexed. Then suspicion seemed to contract the muscles around her eyes again. 'Everyone can, no?'

That was what I had been led to believe too. 'But no one in this place talks,' I said and immediately regretted the tone I had used. At the same time I resented the implication that the surliness I had encountered everywhere was, in some way, my fault. Blood rushed to my face.

She saw that and suppressed a smile. The skin, stretched thin, trembled. 'You must be the tourist at Palm Beach?'

I thought I detected a note of disdain in her tone and, for a minute, I was the one without words. I was not a tourist. At least that was not how I saw myself. Neither was I a native. My categories were different and seemed too difficult to explain to her. I was a man in search of a father, or perhaps in search of himself. The same as everybody else, but on a journey that seemed longer. I told her instead that her doves were the first birds I'd seen since I had landed, even though I had heard there were birds everywhere on the island.

She picked up the empty cage and shook her head, turning glum. 'That was before war changed our nature here.' Her eyes darted around, away from the pond, as if to show me the consequences: the sparse scattering of etiolated flowers under the stooped grey trees. 'Now you have to search hard to find anything beautiful.'

I remember feeling some serious misgivings then about what my father might have been involved in and the true nature of my peculiar inheritance. But what could I do? Despite what she said, I thought the glow in her face was beautiful. I watched dewdrops form on the skin around her mouth and on the slopes of her nose. Sunlight turned them into gems. She was unlike anybody else I had ever seen. Slim and small, she seemed to possess all the space around her. Her face drew everything into it. I didn't want her to move. I wanted to see the shape of the smile she had hidden; to retrieve it for myself.

I can think of a thousand things to say now but then, stammering over every other word, I floundered. I tried to explain that I had come looking for something. My lost soul perhaps, I said, half-jokingly, trying to mask my confusion.

She cheered up at that and almost laughed. 'I can see that.'

I smiled, wanting to encourage her. Wanting more. For a moment it seemed possible, and that everything would work out right. Then the surface of the pond darkened. I looked up at the clouds that had appeared above us. When I turned back to say something to her, she had gone.

The trees and the bushes around seemed undisturbed. I felt depleted. I didn't know what I had done wrong; perhaps I shouldn't have tried to joke about the soul, things spiritual. For some this was, once, an island of the devout. I searched for some mark – a footprint, crushed grass, anything – but it was as though she had never been there.

In the end I returned the way I had come, trudging slower and slower.

By the time I got to the hotel the sun's last beads had seeped out of the sky. I found an old deckchair and took it out to the Sundowner Hut overlooking the pier where the boat had docked a week earlier. The sea rolled from dark burgundy to a lunar blue, erasing the crossing I had made and nudging me back to the reasons that lay behind it.

My father died somewhere in this jungle when I was still a child. My mother took her own life, far from home, not long after. I felt I had never really known either of them; they had hardly ever been around and I had to make do. I grew up with my grandparents, believing I should stay close to home. From an early age I learned to be ultra-cautious. My grandparents themselves had breathed the air of diverse places, but when they spoke of their itinerants' history, I saw only trails of migration that seemed either cruel or futile: the pointless effects of a wayward gene.

My grandfather had been an instructor in a small Chertsey flying school on the edge of London but he had retired long before I was born and was, for me, always an old man with silver hair lining a cloudy brown face; his gentle hands constantly tending his garden, slowing the frenzy of the encroaching city and patiently calming my earliest fears. He passed away when I was twelve. That was harder to take than my parents' desertions. Cleo, my grandmother, was the only one who stayed to see me through. She would make pancakes and bake me banana bread, or ginger cake, every Sunday; once a month re-create Eldon's special fried pork curry. Delicacies to remind me of my antecedents in the wider world beyond the windswept shale and shingle of our South Downs coast. She was a strong, quiet woman with clear beliefs. 'You have them with you, inside you, for always, child,' she would say to console me. 'You will find you have all you need.' Not long after I left school, she died. I drifted a little, trying to ease the hurt, looking for companionship; someone, or something, to hold close.

By my early twenties, I decided the life of a recluse would comfort me more; release me from the recurrence of loss, the delusions of communal life. My strength, I believed in those days, lay in my reticence. I sold the old house and moved into a cheap flat, far from any airport, beyond the crowded flight paths I had lived under as a child. It had no garden, not even a window-box. I wanted things to stand still. I didn't have to do any work and indulged only in secluded, solitary recreations. Like many of my dispirited, isolated neighbours I lived a life of junk, grease and sloth.

Then, about nine months ago – a lifetime ago it seems now – there was an infestation of mice in my cramped bachelor kitchen. A cold snap must have brought them in. I found a trail of droppings by the bread bin and more around the toaster. I had to get rid of the pests but I didn't want to use poison; I didn't want bloated carcasses rotting in some damp corner like those by the bottle-bank outside the municipal library. I decided to drive them away instead, unharmed. I had a go with a broom and brush, clearing out every cupboard in the flat.

That was when I found my lodestar: an antiquated video cassette with my father's name printed on the label followed by the year, 1998. It was in a cardboard box in which I had dumped the few remaining mementoes from my grandparents' house, my childhood props: a bird-watcher's guidebook, a couple of young ornithologists' annuals, a collection of cult CDs and dub poetry, geek software. Things I had not been able to look at for years.

Inside the video case I discovered a note addressed to my mother but written, it seemed, as much for me then as now. Three decades late, in the cold winter light of my scoured London flat, I read the letter, the numbness inside me thawing to its irresistible call. In the days that followed I read it so many times, the neat, precise writing became inscribed in me.

Darling,

I am sorry I have to delay my return again, but there is a lot to be done following the attack last month. As usual everyone is galvanised here only after a bomb explodes. It lasts for a couple of weeks, and then everything sinks back into the same old morass it had been before. But by the summer I should be able to leave the island. So do book that gite. It won't be like here, but it will be good to be all together again, wherever.

Until then I am glad Marc is happily settled with the Grands, and that you can join your team. As you say, it is only for two weeks this time and then nothing again until the Palermo conference in May. Marc will be fine. He has to learn.

Guess what I bought last weekend? A video-camera! I thought it was a good chance to make some clips for you to see what it is really like here now.

I find it so much easier to talk into the camera than to write, but there hasn't been enough time to use it much. I am sending you this first cassette, as a starter.

Someday, when this business is all over, I really want to bring Marc here with me. I want to show him this place the way Dad did with me on that wonderful trip I had with him all those years ago. I found something then, locked inside myself, although it took a journey of love, years later, to release it. I want Marc to understand why I had to come back, and what I found on this island, because I hope, one day, that he will too.

My love to you both,

Lee.

He had found a dream, even though Eldon had always insisted his – ours – was an island where dreamers often have to destroy their dreams, if they are not to be destroyed by them.

I had never been shown the video by my mother or by my grandmother. Perhaps they couldn't bear to. Perhaps they both feared the effect it would have on me. But all alone in my flat I watched it over and over with a mounting desire to break out. *Marc, you would love it* . . . he promised from every fugitive frame. Listening to the voice of my father calling me from the emerald island that had once been his father's home, the place of my parents' conjugal romance, I realised I too had to go to find something more. There was nothing for me in London.

I handed my flat over to a management agency and put my few remaining possessions into long-term storage. All my other assets I converted into cash deposits. The man at the bank warned me, 'Global access does not include bunkers in war-zones, you realise, don't you?' I explained that the island I was going to was not an actual war zone any more and that, in any case, I could easily carry enough dollars to last me six months or more out there. My young banker did not look convinced. 'Nobody knows what goes on in those trouble spots.'

I said that was precisely why I wanted to go. Within three weeks I was on my way.

That evening, rocking on my Palm Beach Hotel deckchair, close to the pulse of a warm sea, I thought about my encounter in the jungle. She was not what I had come looking for, but her appearance made me feel I might discover something of what I had been missing.

The next day I was impatient to get back to the duckweed pond. I wanted to hear what else she could tell me. Or already, perhaps, I just wanted to be with her. I couldn't be sure she'd return; my only hope was to be there at the same time as before.

After the usual bland lunch at the hotel, I set off back into a world of field glasses and feathers. The sun was piercing, but I didn't care.

When I reached the pond, I noticed the water was rimmed with scum. A small lily had opened near where we had stood the day before. It had some colour: a tinge of red on the lower petals. The weeds on the bank also seemed a little darker. I tried to locate the tree that her birds had flown to, but there were no fruits to be seen anywhere.

There were no clouds, no wind. The heat seemed more severe than before. I sat in the shade to wait. I had a flask of drinking water with me this time, but it didn't help. There was not much I could do to relieve the burning I felt inside.

I tried again to meditate; to balance the heat inside and outside my body. I was close to a kind of equilibrium, when the thrashing of wings startled me. I twisted around. She stood there just as I had remembered her. A radiant face, her whole body held taut. Only her hair seemed a little more tousled. She had the same cage open; another dove was flapping in her hand. This time she was not surprised to see me.

'You disappeared,' I complained, rising up to my feet.

She lifted the bird up to her face and came close to me. 'So? You are back, no?'

I wanted her to talk some more, yet I could say nothing to encourage her. I was worried I might blurt out something stupid again. I felt she was looking at me, assessing me, even while she soothed the bird. In her hair I noticed a scrap of yellow. As I reached to remove the leaf, it unfolded into a small butterfly and fluttered towards the water.

She shrank back. 'What are you doing?'

'Nothing,' I said. 'I thought there was something stuck.' My hand felt detached. It floated between us. A stick in limbo. I pictured my father meeting my mother somewhere on the coast of this same island. What did he say standing in sand?

'Why have you come?' she asked.

I couldn't tell her it was because of some old home video. I couldn't even say that it was because I wanted to see her again.

'There's nothing left here, you know?'

'What about those?' I nodded at her cage.

She sighed and seemed to relax a little. 'The birds?'

'Where are they from?'

'My ashram.' She paused.

I told her that there were ashrams where I came from too, but they were meant for people stressed out by city life.

'Your city?'

'London.' I hesitated.

She nodded with a small grimace as though I had said enough for her to imagine the rest. She then told me how her mother had wanted to create an ashram for all the birds of the air because she believed they were the souls of us all. Emerald doves were her favourites. 'Come, I'll show you a nest.' She took my hand in hers and led me towards

21

the trees as though it was the most natural thing in the world to do.

I had never felt a touch like hers. Her skin was soft, yet the grip firm. I looked at her small hand; her fingers wrapped around the ends of mine. The knuckles were smooth. A greenish vein swelled on the back of her hand; her wrist was chafed where her bracelet had rubbed it. I could feel the life in her.

I curled my fingers to let the blood in them flow closer to hers.

All along the forest path dark ferns genuflected as she brushed past. Noli-me-tangere, she said they were called. By an old mudbank she pointed out a litter of pigs she said she had released to the wild and, in the distance, her favourite trees. 'Over there, in the older jungle where nobody goes, is my farm.' She pressed her finger to my lips leaving me a crystalline trace to savour from the giddy whorls on her skin. 'Illegal. Nobody knows.' She nearly smiled again.

I was intrigued. She didn't say any more about it; I could see she wasn't ready to take me there yet.

She let go of me and used both her hands to clear a way through the bushes. I smothered her small sandal marks with my larger treads, watching the curve of her neck as she bent her head to go under some branches. I had to stoop lower to follow her. Her bare foot straightened, ahead of me, as she stood on tiptoe to climb over a fallen tree trunk. The bone of her brown ankle peeped from under the denim as she lifted her leg over. 'Come on, this way,' she urged.

Then, in a clump of straw saplings, she uncovered a secret woven nest for me. 'This is one of the halfway houses.' She blew a small blue fluffy feather up into the air; there was nothing else in it. She explained that it was where she nursed the birds who were slow to regain their foraging instincts.

Pulling the branches back over the nest, she concealed it as before. Further on, underneath the ironwood tree, she found the corpse of one which had come to grief. She picked up the little sunbird and folded in its wings. Her face dipped, solemn but not tearful. 'Oh-oh,' she clucked like someone who had grown too fast into the world. 'It is not easy for them, you know, to learn to be free.'

I felt a tingle run down my spine. I had come to learn too. Perhaps the eroded coast I had reached was, after all, the right place to start on this island. Watching her bury the bird under a small mound of leaves I wondered, was this the person who could show me what I really needed to know?

She covered our tracks and dusted her hands, looking around thoughtfully. Then she turned to me and said it was time to take me back. 'The path can be tricky, you know, when it gets dark. Sometimes the night patrols are trigger-happy.'

I wasn't sure whether I should hold her hand again. I swung mine close as we sauntered out into the open, but she seemed too busy thinking about military manoeuvres to notice.

When we reached the edge of the village, she said, 'I must go now.'

'When can I see you again?' I asked.

'Tomorrow. Same place, the same time again. I have lots more birds to bring.' She looked up at the darkened sky above me, filling it with wings. A nervous quiver ran down her throat. In my mind I turned it to that laugh from the previous day, still hovering inside her, waiting to break free.

I felt hollow after she had gone, emptier than before. The

breeze was warm, but there was something cold under my skin as if I carried winter in my bones. I felt I had crossed a line that split the world and me; I was both lost and found at the same time. 'Sindbad was the bugger', my grandfather used to say tapping his head with his finger, 'who showed us how we forget what we should remember – the dangers of the voyage – and remember what we should forget: the place we must leave behind.' Eldon always had some dictum or other to fix every moment in its place. I had none of my own and, at that moment, I couldn't even tell the sea from the shore.

I made my way, reluctantly, to the entrance of the hotel. The building seemed to have sunk further into the ground. The lights were low. The gates which were usually open had been locked. It didn't worry me. I was too absorbed with what was happening inside me. I clanked the chain several times and, finally, a young security guard appeared. I didn't recognise him but he smiled shyly when he saw me. He too seemed to know who I was. He slung his short-barrelled gun over his shoulder and fumbled with the padlock.

'Late, sir,' he remarked with a surreptitious eagerness.

'I was out walking,' I replied, surprised to find yet another person keen to speak. What was going on? 'Why is it locked so early?' There had been no curfew as such before.

He grinned, dragging back the gate and letting me through. 'Today's order, sir. Power is down.' He looked pleased at being so informative.

'I haven't seen you before. Are you new?' I asked.

His gawky face opened again into a broken smile. One of his teeth was missing. 'Just came, sir.' He swayed in youthful enthusiasm. The gun slipped off his shoulder. He grabbed at it, but then the chain slithered out of his hand pulling a bag from his belt and spilling its contents around his feet.

24

I picked up the gun, a crude stripped-down assault rifle, while he scrabbled around for the other bits. I asked him his name.

'Nirali, sir.' There was a dimple in his chin that rolled when he moved his lips.

'I'm glad you can talk, Nirali,' I said, handing him his gun. 'Nobody else in this hotel seems to want to.'

'Yes, sir.' He grinned again and tucked the weapon under his arm. 'I like to, sir.'

'Good.' I was pleased at the way things were turning out. 'My name, by the way, is Marc.'

'Yes, sir. Goodnight, sir. See you tomorrow, sir.'

'Goodnight, Nirali.'

At the deserted front desk I rang the bell and waited. After a little while a familiar ghoulish figure ambled out of a back room, holding up a lantern. I asked for my key and room service.

'We can give only sandwich tonight,' he grumbled. 'Shrimp paste.' He turned the wick of his lamp down in obeisance to some malevolent shadow behind him.

'That's fine,' I shrugged. 'Shrimp paste will do fine.'

In my room I lit a candle and waited for the meagre meal to arrive. I snapped open a beer and tried to reflect on the changes that had taken place. The dreary hotel no longer bothered me. The air was clearing. Nirali, the security guard, reminded me of the picture I had of my father. Something in that uneven enthusiastic smile, an echo perhaps, as in his name.

But her name meant even more. Her name, she had said, was Uva, and I said it again to myself: Uva. I recognised it as the name of my grandfather's favourite strong black tea, but she told me it was the name of a region of high mountains, the home of venerable old gods and forest folk in perennial rebellion. 'We have always had to fight for our freedom,' she had grinned, 'against waves and waves of your brass-balled colonisers.'

The following afternoon she was there again, just as she had promised. She had her cage with her as before, but she looked different. Dressed up, even though the T-shirt and jeans were the same. I stared, keeping my distance, unsure where we had left off the previous evening; where we stood now. She had scrunched her hair back and wore a necklace that looked like a string of teeth.

'Fangs?' I asked.

She looked puzzled.

'Around your neck? Are those fangs?'

She looked down at her chest and broke into a laugh, making me laugh too, not knowing why nor caring.

'They're beads, no? Wooden beads only.'

'Oh, I see.' I felt hot, clammy, searching for something else to say. 'Birds. Those are more birds?' The words leapt out.

She twirled the beads with her fingers, feeling for their shapes.

I reached for her cage, but she moved it away. 'No. Wait.'

I waited, remembering herons by a river, spring flowers adrift, the hasty ejaculations of early youth.

She opened the cage and a small brown salaleena whistled. Uva squinted and pursed her lips in reply. The bird stuck its head out, peered one way and then the other, and then flew out. I watched the muscles in her face ripen.

I didn't know what I wanted to happen next. I was not a youngster any more. If I had seen her on the

Twickenham bridge, casting bread, I would have heaved back my shoulders and walked on, assuming our worlds would never even rhyme. But by her green duckweed pond I felt I had entered another universe. I stood there giftless and gormless.

She looked up at me, quizzically. 'Have you never seen salaleenas before?'

I tried, incoherently, to catch the threads of our failing conversation.

'Have you?' she repeated. 'No?'

Finally, with that last tilted syllable her tongue irrevocably untied mine; the tide in her, and in myself too, released more words then than I thought I knew. Something burst inside me and out. Thrilled, I told her how wonderful it was to see her. How my whole journey, not just into the jungle, but to the island itself, now made sense. How I felt my life and the whole gloomy place had altered since I met her. How limes flowered and birds flew and everything had come alive. How not only salaleenas, but even the security guards were now keen to talk. I told her about Nirali, wondering if he might be one of her flock.

She ran her tongue under her lips. 'You have any idea of where you really are?'

I felt stung by the accusation.

'We live in a state of terror. Can't you see it? It is not that we are just a little shabby here. We have had to adjust our thresholds. Abuse our minds as we do our bodies when we have to control pain.'

Yes, I wanted to say, yes, I know how bad it is. I wanted to say I was sorry that I could not feel her pain, or anybody else's. It was not my fault that we all have only our own.

'Your Nirali is a lucky innocent still,' she continued,

27

'but they will bend him, you see, when he is ready to join a squad.'

'Nirali?' I shook my head, trying to comprehend what she was suggesting. 'No, he wouldn't join. He doesn't even like to be a guard. He'd rather work inside at the desk, or even as a waiter.'

She half-closed her eyes as though to stop some cerebral pain. I would have stopped it for her, if only I could. Nirali was not the one I wanted to talk about. I wondered what would happen if I kissed her. Would the world change then, at least for us? At that moment all I wanted from my life, from everything around me and before me, coalesced into her. I remember a sort of haze that rippled with her every breath. My father's ghost, Eldon's shadow, my disjointed past and all the corruption around us receded from my mind as I gazed at her. I realised that all I had been looking for was there in front of me. I tightened my lips, as though that alone would be enough. Then, unable to stop, I kissed her. I could only think of touching her lips. Supplanting that air warmed by her breath with the lightest brush of my thinnest skin. Nothing else.

She kissed me back.

The hours moved swiftly then. I wanted time to slow down with her; speed up when I was without her. Change its nature to coincide with ours.

The very next evening she took me beyond the ash rocks where the stone-curlews used to nest. She showed me the path of the moon and lit a fire on the beach between three coconut palms and a bunch of lime trees. She threw nutmeg and ola leaves in the flames and let the smoke clothe her. I watched her bow, like a magician, into her own pubis and vanish briefly, singing, into a floating veil. My arms ached as they ache even now; in the small of my back a muscle was stretched taut. Smoke compressed the breath in my lungs, and I choked for the want of her skin around me, her voice inside me, her heart's beat next to mine, changing mine.

Within just days I felt I had known her for ever; her eyes, her mouth, her arms wide open, encircling, echoed everywhere. 'Come with me,' she murmured even in her cloud-warmed sleep. Taking my arm – eager to go, eager to hold – she walked me to the beach under a sky of laughing stars. She drew runes along the edge of the ocean dragging her toes in the warm, wet sand. She talked and talked to me, constructing a citadel of hope. I told her about my grandfather's Eden and she said that she had heard that there was once a whole region full of butterflies and flowers – Samandia – but nobody went that far into the blighted south any more. 'You'll have to find somewhere else,' she said 'make your own Eden.'

'I know,' I said. 'It's not his I want, but ours.'

When we made love, my life rocked. She'd trace with her fingers the seams of my legs, the ridges of my back, my deepest wishbone rising like a swallow, and I would touch hers rippling under a skin strained by the notes of a mangled melody.

The next day she held me close and told me, 'I want you to see what they do to control us.'

We had to walk two kilometres up the coast to get to the place she wanted to show me: a charred shell of a house with the ground around it black and full of cinders.

'I knew the family that lived here,' she said. 'They were meant to grow only bitter gourd and radish for the market, but they had young children and got some sugarcane going. It was against the rules. One day the military came and saw the boy eating sugarcane. They tried to catch him to beat him, but he ran away. The soldiers couldn't find him so they burnt the whole place down.' She led me to where some new shoots were growing through. 'But they can't win. Look, the cane is coming up again. It will be taller and sweeter and give us all strength.'

'What happened to the family?' I asked.

Uva stared down at the ground. 'The boy got away, I guess.'

Back on the beach, later, she brought out a perfectly shaped mango from a cotton sack. 'Try this beauty I stole from a District Commander's garden. From a very old protected tree. Even they – their leaders – know the best comes from what is to be found, no? Not forced.' She cut the mango into two pools of set sun, running the blade of her butterfly knife – a sharp sliver of steel hidden in twin hinged sticks of black wood and oxidised copper – right up against the swollen seed inside.

I admired her pluck, the hidden strength of what she described as her natural filaments.

'My genes,' she smiled. 'The women in my family have always nurtured our inner wings. My mother, Rosa, became a legend here.'

'What was she? An eco-warrior?'

'More a kind of ornithologist. Like you, looking everywhere for the bird of paradise.' She glanced at me, covertly, to check my reaction, and then broke into a chuckle.

I reached for her, but my fingers barely brushed her tarsus as she rose. Her heels drummed me completely to her song.

'Would you ever leave this place? Break free from all the hassle,' I asked her afterwards.

'That would be impossible,' she said.

Above the sea-line the light was eroding fast. Uva mopped the fruit juice and our commingled resin off the groundsheet with a piece of silk. She sniffed at it and smiled to herself. She folded up the sheet into a tiny square and buckled it to her bag. Then suddenly she was gone, leaving behind only the scent of her ardour.

The next time I saw her was when she turned up on her tricycle. She came with a big box full of fresh eggs and untainted fruit – rambutan, guava, star-apple – all concealed under a tray of buff envelopes. She rode up to the terrace and rang her bell. I was in a hammock outside. She pushed back her hair and tossed me a clutch of rambutan. 'Catch.' The rest of the fruit she handed to the sweeper sprawled by the pool. The eggs she gave to the cook, in the kitchen, to make into an omelette. All their faces seemed to lift each time she came around. She even managed to get the hotel jeep for our use and promised to take me to one of the ancient ruined cities that the military, apparently, no longer bothered with. She chortled when I asked whether it was dangerous for her to bend the rules of the hotel so freely. It worried me even though by then I was pretty much settled in the place.

'Why? I am allowed to come here. Deliveries is what I do. Your lady mail. It's just that I am not meant to be a guest here.' She grinned. 'But tonight maybe I will stay with you. The people who do the work here like me. I give them fruit whenever I can, no? Tusker, in the bar, is the only spy, and he is much too fond of my sweet sapadillo to report me. Even Nirali, whenever I see him, says he likes to talk only to you.' She laughed effortlessly and ran her fingers over mine.

She made me rejoice despite the dour surroundings. I wanted to hold her hand for ever. 'Mutual self-interest, is it?'

Her smile ran amok briefly, before vanishing from her face. Her bright eyes dampened. The light sank as if into a pit. 'We all lived *for* each other once, not in need of each other,' she replied. 'The world was made out of love. You have to believe that, don't you?'

Although younger than me, she seemed to have a grasp of the past which reached far beyond the confusion of mine.

I heard the baying of hunting dogs in the distance. 'What are they hunting?' I asked her.

Her face darkened, 'I hope not your Nirali already.'

I felt a chill inside. I hadn't seen him for two days.

Breakfast came and we ate silently. Then, just as I started to ask her more, we heard a motorbike puttering up the drive. 'Hide everything. Pretend I was never here,' she hissed and slipped into the garden. Fortunately we had finished the omelette and the fruit. I chucked my serviette on the table, over her cutlery and glass of juice. There was nothing else I could do. I heard someone march around the reception area and then a man burst out onto the terrace. He was armed: the gun was in its holster and he carried a crash helmet in one hand. He whipped a pair of dark glasses over his eyes and moved hastily around the tables. I looked at him as steadily as I could. He came up to my table and stared at the rumpled serviette. He slid a finger inside the neck of his brown tunic as if to let air into a suffocating chest. 'Tourist?'

I nodded, not sure whether I should reach for my passport.

'You see the security guard?'

'Which one?' I asked, trying to think of some way to protect Nirali.

'Young one. Broken tooth.'

I made an empty gesture with my hands. 'Could be the guy who went out in the dinghy.'

He stared at me, trying to draw out something more. I resisted. After a moment he spun around and headed for the boathouse. A weight dropped from my shoulders; my legs, under the table, felt weak.

Once the man had left on his motorbike, Uva returned, her face animated.

'He was looking for Nirali. I tried to put him off,' I said.

'I know.' Uva's eyes hardened. 'He is an executioner. If he'd seen me, he'd think I was hiding Nirali.'

'Are you?' I asked.

'No. I gave him the name of a friend in the city. I couldn't risk the farm. I don't let anyone come near.'

'Not even me?'

She didn't reply immediately. She could trust me by now, surely, I thought. 'Maybe in a day or two. When I can be sure we won't be tracked.' She took my hand. 'I do want you there. I want you to see it.'

She stayed with me that night; she said the hotel was probably the safest place now that the man had made his visit. It was not quite how I expected it to be.

Soon after daybreak we heard a helicopter circling, searching the coast. We kept out of sight. Later, in the afternoon, while I was trying to sleep I thought I heard shots, but I couldn't be sure.

After dark, we had dinner outside on the terrace again. Tusker, dressed in an old black and white suit, served us; despite the circumstances, I thought he looked quite comic gliding in and out of the shadows. 'A tropical goth,' I whispered to Uva, but she didn't know what I was on about.

The following morning the cook informed Uva that he had heard the executioner had left the area.

'What does that mean?' I asked her. I didn't know how easily they gave up.

'Can't say.'

'Can we go out, you think?'

'Maybe, but not too far.'

I suggested the small cove I had found when I first explored the ramparts behind the village.

She said that should be OK.

When we got there, the sand looked good. The sea was bright blue. Even the sun seemed a little kinder.

I found a shady spot near the wall. 'Come, we can lay your mat here,' I called out.

Uva was down by the water. She was turning over something with her foot. She looked distressed.

'What's wrong?' I went over, thinking she'd found another bird.

She kicked at the wet sand. 'They must have caught him,' she said.

'Who?'

She showed me the empty shell of a cartridge she had picked up. There were two more in the sand. 'They do it on

34

the beach. The executions. They must have shot him here last night. The blood just drains away.' Her voice trembled slightly. 'This sand here never stains, you know, no matter how much blood is spilled.'

I tried to imagine Nirali's awkward eager face. I couldn't. The sea filled my eyes.

The next day she took me to her farm. We had to go through what seemed to me impenetrable jungle. When we finally reached her secret vale, I was amazed. There were clumps of bamboo and banana, tall avocado trees, shrubs full of berries and lantana growing everywhere. She had small nurseries of various crops, chicken runs and animal shelters hidden in between. 'The aviaries are in those trees.' She pointed to the jungle behind a small hut made of mud.

'You did all this?'

'Why not?'

'By yourself?'

'I have a network of friends, but they are not all farmers. We each do our own thing. One day, maybe, we will learn to learn from each other about something more than an ugly war.'

I told her that's what I wanted too. I told her about my parents, and grandparents, and how their lives had been shaped by wars that were not their own.

She took me into the hut. 'My father was in the Forestry Commission before our last big war blew everything apart. He hated the politics and bigotry in the service; he dropped out to make an alternative life with my mother. He was an idealist and an artist. He made things. All he ever wanted was to create a sanctuary for us. Evergrowing. You know, the very first sanctuaries on earth were on this island.' Her eyes misted over. 'He'd say, "The edicts of the past are what we, in this place, so progressively forget," you understand?'

Her mother, Uva said, came from a family who had cleared forests and planted imperial crops for three generations. Probably Eldon's coconut kings: making money; taking, never giving. Uva's mother had felt compelled to foster all the fruits of the earth in recompense. 'She taught me to farm in a different way – with real care.' Uva's mother had found a place high up in the hills, unspoiled, from where she could reintroduce the natural world into the overexploited cashlands of their denuded province. Her mother wanted these to return to a richer jungle rather than the leached scrubland that retreating global markets and destitute governments left in their wake. 'My father built with her a home using tiles like in the olden times, and protected the wilderness there as a refuge for the birds, the animals, the insects, the plants that were being destroyed by all those profiteers. My parents believed that the world should be an interdependent living thing. That was their dream.' She joined her hands together in the shape of a prayer and breathed into the hollow between her palms. 'But the new warlords and their cronies were the only ones to thrive here. They grew fatter and fatter – feeding on the greed, the mistrust and the endless war. They destroyed everything, no? The ones on this side of the island took the cat's eye for themselves, in the east they took the toad's head for their symbol.'

'So your father didn't fight?' Was he like Eldon I wondered. I compared them, silently: Eldon's chosen path of pacifism, his mask of spiritual detachment, his harking back to ancients, his desire for things to grow.

Uva watched me for a while as if searching for a sign of my return. Then, when she was sure I was with her again, she continued. 'War here, like everywhere else, was once about land and identity. But after the death cloud in the south everything changed. You see, we were reshaped by gangsters into new collectives held together only by conscription. You could say myopia, no? Not language, not religion, not any of those outmoded notions of nation. After so many years of fighting, violence became ingrained into our way of life. So now we have only thugs for politicians and tyranny in every tribe. Killers everywhere. You know, as a ranger my father could kill too – he knew how to hunt – but he never killed for vengeance. He didn't do it for politics, or for pleasure like these goombahs.'

'Where did he draw the line?'

'In his heart, no? When he hunted, he would do it only out of love. He'd hunt a leopard to save a deer, and sometimes a deer, to save the herd. He would cull if it was necessary but for their sake, not ours. He hoped if he could provide a haven, it would be enough.'

When she said that, I thought of my father; was that what he believed too? Was it my father, in the end, who shared the same dream? I couldn't figure it out. I didn't know how to put it into words, then, that would make sense to anyone.

The next few days, every morning we would go to the farm and collect fruit and eggs. She'd tend to her animals and birds, while I prepared a salad or a sandwich out of cucumber, tomato and village bread. In the afternoons we'd lie in the shade, or on her wooden bed, and explore each other's lives: touching, talking, discovering with our tongues whatever our lips could not.

She told me how lucky she was that her parents had given her a taste for freedom, and I told her how in my case I had

37

to thank my grandparents. I'd try to explain the conflict of loyalties I felt in the past, but the problem did not seem to matter that much any more.

One afternoon, when we were gathering our things to return to the hotel for the night, I noticed a small figurine on her bedside table. The room was dark, even during the day, and I had to take it up to the window to see it properly. It turned out to be a carving of a creature half-man, half-bird. The body was painted green, the wings gold and the human arms decorated with tiny copper bracelets.

'Where did you get this?' I asked Uva.

'My father was an artist, I told you. He made it. He was fascinated by the idea that the mythical creatures we imagine might come from some memory of our evolution. This one is his version of a kind of garuda. A bird becoming human.'

'I suppose the story of the man who flew too close to the sun is another?'

She took the carving from me and placed it back in the shadows. 'He thought they were all connected, you see. Even the sun was once seen as a bird.'

'Like us?' I tried to remember how far Eldon went with his theories, but then Uva pulled me outside to show me a pair of bush-larks courting. They flew up repeating their high notes to each other and then parachuted down, legs dangling and wings uplifted.

'But we can't do that, can we?' she said.

I stretched out my arms. 'Sure we can. In my family . . .'

She giggled at that and tickled me. 'Let's see then, let's see.'

★   ★   ★

A few days later, nestled with me in bed, she told me how the night her mother, her father and her home were destroyed, she was pierced in three places: in her heart, her head and her soul. She said she became determined then to carry on with their vision in secret, in disguise, in any way she could. Her voice dropped low in her thin wilting throat when she spoke of her war, as though the enemy was within her now. 'I don't want to talk any more about it. I can still taste that graphite dust in my mouth. What's gone must one day come back.' Her eyelids drooped, trapped in her parents' web of unravelled hope.

'How will you know you have done what you have to do here?'

'I only want to keep their spirit alive. I'll know when I am no longer needed. There will be birds everywhere – my mother's emerald doves at least – and clouds of butterflies like flowers in the air. We will each have a garden of our own.' She half-opened her eyes. 'How will you know that you have found what you are looking for?'

'I already have.'

'What? You think that just because we can jiggle our hips together everything is all right?' She squinted hard, screwing up her face. 'Look at this seedy hotel you are stuck in, will you? You remember how it looked to you at first? What I said to you about how we survive? Just think about my muddy little hut you like so much to wallow in. That pathetic plot of sweet potato I have to dig. If we think this is the best we can do then we will have become just like them: forgetting pain and remembering nothing.' Her words grated. But I thought I could remember everything I needed to then, as I can now: my arrival, her pond, our first conversations. The way she wafted through the hotel and tumbled into my room. Our walks together on the beach, through the forests. Her camouflaged crops, the lantana blossom, her chickens, her pigs and her goats. The coir mattress on her vermilion bed, her body in my arms, every fold and fissure within her. I could remember the sun, the moon and the stars. And far away my grandfather's garden and my journey from his to hers.

It is enough, I wanted to say then. It was more than I had ever dreamed was possible.

She had shown me everything that mattered on the coast, except the city. She said she didn't like Maravil, even though her closest friends were there.

'Doing their own thing?'

'Yes, traders, and . . . Jaz.' She said he was the best friend she'd ever had. 'He is always able to make me feel good when I'm down.'

'I'd like to meet him then,' I said.

She laughed. 'You wouldn't understand him.' She described Jaz as Maravil's most erogenous creature; ensconced in the exclusive Carnival Mall – a restricted leisure centre – he could do practically anything except set himself free. 'No one can reach beneath his surface,' she explained.

I said I'd like to try.

'The mall is for pass-holders only, but you need an official ID even to get into the city – unless it is a market day. You have to be registered by birth or trade. Or branded like one of their captives.'

'What about foreigners? I thought there were some there?'

'Sometimes they keep foreigners like pets. Usually some dumb diplomat who steps outside their special enclave, or one of the rare tourists from the quarantine north resort who goes too far.' She grinned. 'They tag you then. You would be free to remain but not to leave our warlord's domain.'

It figured. I told her Eldon's story. 'He used to say there is a long tradition of washed-up tourists suffering what he called inescapable hospitality here: the Argonauts, seventeenth-century sailors. The odd globetrotter, you know?' Only then, in the retelling, did it strike me. 'I think he really believed that in any country it is only the foreigner who can feel a genuine sense of belonging, of arrival, of arriving home. We become committed: perpetually enchanted or permanently detained.' I began to wonder about ancient mariners, traders and travellers. But was he right? We were all foreigners once. And what about the history of slavery? Enforced migration? Escape and exile? Uva? The stuff that was going on around us? It's not just a matter of who you are, or where you are; surely how you got there must make a difference? What he meant, perhaps, was people like himself. Was that what I was beginning to feel too? 'Perhaps people like me,' I added. 'We feel committed.'

She laughed. 'Desire, my love, is all you feel.'

She parted my tight curls and moistened a path of enchantment with her silver-studded tongue from my throat down to my navel. Then, in her retreat, she undid the weave of her homespun cloth exposing every curve and cleft of her uncoated flesh, the whole spine of her hidden plume.

Her body was always warmer than mine. In the early hours of the morning the warmth drew me to her under our gossamer net. And when we had water to shower with, her warm surface melted mine into a sea of concupiscence rippled by her bluish tongue. Her silver anklet would pierce my back; I would hear the sound of feathers pressed to her perfume, buried between her stride, her fingers tugging at my hair, her whole body buoyed up in my hands. But I failed her when she needed me most. Too slow, too uncertain; my hopes that day, at our palm beach, were what let me down.

Uva had gone back to the farm, alone, to collect our daily basket of fruit; I was in my room trying to make sense of a map she had managed to get for me. Four weeks had passed and I was beginning to feel I should make an effort to see a bit more of the region inland, even if I couldn't get to all the places I had first wanted to. Locating the hotel on the local map and matching the details to the older one I had brought with me on the boat was proving difficult. I had barely managed to identify the region where Eldon's Eden, perhaps even Lee's graveyard, might be when she rushed in and locked the door behind her. Her eyes were swollen, her voice shrivelled. 'Kill me, Marc, before I really become like one of those bastards.'

I tried to soothe her, but she twisted around and unstrapped her butterfly knife. 'Quickly,' she hissed, 'now, before it's too late.' I had to grasp her hand and force her fingers apart as only a lover could, tearing the skin on the web between her thumb and forefinger.

'Let go. It's my knife.' Her face was thin, tense; watching me while watching out. 'They've destroyed the hatchery, my seedlings, the nursery, everything.'

Was that smoke in her hair? My hand seemed to burn where I touched her, but I did not let go.

'I want to kill every one of them. Tusker, that bastard first . . .' She bit her lip until blood appeared.

I wanted then, as I do now, to lick it clean; staunch the

flow. Her pulse was in my hands. She dug into my skin with her fingers. I untangled the strands of her long warm hair. 'I don't believe in death,' the rich comforting voice of my childhood's guardian echoed in my throat. 'You know that.'

She pulled away from me and moved slowly to the window. Beyond the bare, parched lawn of the hotel garden, the beach cowered as the surf smashed the shore, splitting each grain of sand against each other. 'They've destroyed the whole farm. All the animals. Every little bird. The hut was blazing. My garuda . . . everything gone. Now they'll be after me.'

I saw again the burnt farmstead she'd shown me, and tried to keep her vale from merging into it in my mind. 'We'd better get to that special enclave in the city, an embassy.'

She stared at me as if I was mad. 'They won't help me. You know secret farmers like me are not their interest. Even Jaz . . .'

'What about that place in the south then, where you said no one goes any more?'

A stray sunbeam lit her eye. 'Samandia? Yes, we might be safe in Samandia.' She wiped her hand across her face. There was ash on her cheek.

I told her to slip out around the side of the hotel and wait by the gate while I fetched the keys to the hotel jeep from the bellboy's box. She nodded, looking for once, a little uncertain. Her breath, warm, tinged with blood, seemed to be still. I left her as I never ever want to leave her again.

When I couldn't find the keys in the box, I stupidly searched all the drawers of the unattended reception desk instead of going into the office straight away. I was in a panic. I wished I hadn't let her keep her knife, given the state she was in. By the time I found the keys and raced to the gate, I was too late. I turned to look back once more at the old hotel and saw a shadow on the terrace raise a gun. I jumped, crying out. The path turned red, the insides of my eyelids redder. An icy chemical flooded the pores of my shoulder before I even felt the puncture of the soldier's dart; a cool, light, feeling of night descending, a curdled sky swelling in my veins. There was pain. My every membrane quivered like a pricked inner ear.

II

MARAVIL

W HEN I regained consciousness, I found myself on a metal bed. It was daylight, and hot. I could see only sky through the small windows of the grey wall opposite. There were ten beds in the ward and one other patient: a small figure with a bandage around his chest. A stout woman in a nurse's uniform guarded the door. I wasn't sure whether I should show I was awake.

I was in a sleeveless smock and there was a small dressing taped to my shoulder. I tried to remember whether I had seen Uva running towards me or away.

A doctor came in, looking rather harassed. He hurried over to the other patient and leafed through the papers on the clipboard dangling at the end of the bed. He said something to the nurse who had followed behind and then scribbled on the board. Then he turned towards me.

He was a young man with a worried face. 'Feeling better?' he asked and checked my pulse.

I asked him where I was, and what had happened.

Using his thumbs he pulled my lower lids down and examined my eyes. 'A minor accident. You've been sedated.' He asked to see my tongue. Then he told me to turn my head to one side on the pillow. I felt him do something with my ear.

'Is that a tag?'

'Think of it as an earring,' he replied. Quickly he removed the dressing from my shoulder. The plaster strips coming off hurt more than whatever he'd done before. He jotted down something on my clipboard too and handed it to the nurse.

Later I was given some bread and radish curry to eat. When I finished, the nurse brought me my clothes. She didn't speak, but it was obvious that I was meant to get dressed. I was then escorted to the doctor's office.

'You'll be taken to your quarters now,' the doctor said, scribbling some more on a pad. He went on to explain that I was not a prisoner, but only temporarily restricted. 'You'll get what you need, until a decision is made. You see, you were an unfortunate obstruction in an incident yesterday.' My dollars and my watch had been confiscated, but he assured me that I would be given a ration of tokens to use in due course. He discharged me into the custody of two soldiers who were lounging outside. 'Your suitcase is in the van already.'

The back of the vehicle had no windows. I couldn't see where we were going. When we stopped and I was let out, I didn't recognise the area at all. It was bleaker and dryer than anywhere I'd been. There was no hint of the sea.

I was led into a compound of concrete cells. Each with one barred window and a metal door. There were about a dozen of them; none of them looked occupied.

A soldier pointed mine out and also showed me the standpipe and the latrine. The other informed me that food

48

would be brought once a day to the sentry-point on the main road at the end of the lane. He used his gun to indicate the direction I should take. 'Come at first whistle.'

'I can walk there?' I asked.

He nodded. 'But fences are electric,' he warned.

After the soldiers left, I saw some dark figures scuttling in and out of another compound, across the way. I tried make some contact, wondering if Uva might be among them, but no one responded. I gave up. I couldn't see any women there, and the men looked as though they belonged to some religious sect. We may not have been in prison but each area was fenced in; theirs did not seem to have a gate opening on to the same dusty lane that mine did. I guessed the only entrance was via the main road, and presumably restricted.

I was still in a state of shock, I suppose, and went to sleep before dark.

The military whistle in the morning was a siren designed to oppress as much as awake. With each passing minute heat rose and the vibrating air thickened. I got myself ready as quickly as I could, but when I stepped out into the lane I felt the sun had already warped the earth. In the phosphorus dust by the gate a big black beetle lay upside-down, its thorax chewed into a crater. I stuck to the edge, walking beneath the trees, a shade or two less in temperature. The border bristled with brittle weeds, clumps of spearheads. In places I could see nests of red termites devouring the earth.

At the sentry-point I found I was the only one there to collect provisions. The soldier on guard pointed some device at my head, presumably to check my ID against his register.

There wasn't much to eat; only bread and a coconut mix

– no fruit, no vegetables, no meat – but I knew it would have to do for the whole day.

On the other side of the main road, I could see the boundary of an army camp. I thought I could feel the ground shudder all morning to the ritual stomp of boots there.

Some time later, the whistle blew again – two blasts – to denote midday, I guessed.

When the sun finally began to drop, I walked down the lane going in the opposite direction to the main road. I found a wood-apple rotting on a barbed wire, and then, at the end of the lane, a shrunken waterhole that reminded me of where I had first seen Uva.

Each day, thereafter, I would go to the waterhole and watch it shrink another crimped ripline, imagining it was her duckweed pond in mourning. Each day, using my pair of ruby binoculars, I would search the trees before the pulping of the sun, looking for an ash dove or another green imperial pigeon, but there were none of her feathered souls anywhere to be seen. I wanted to believe they would reappear, re-adorned, singing for a greener world, as she must, but all I ever saw was the erratic dive of a single mutilated tree-frog, or a stray fox-bat riding a heatwave. I had to accept the compound was much further inland than I had ever been with her.

Every evening I would wait by the mudrim for seepal-flares to light and only then retrace my steps to the concrete compound, dreaming sometimes that I might find myself returning to the safe suburb where I had been born.

On my tenth evening at the waterhole, watching the sun sink, I saw a pair of stretched leather wings collapse midway to nowhere; a fox snout swung. A sharp explosion echoed and the creature back-flapped, stalled, fell two cubits before regaining the lift needed to glide in on a lower warmstream to the dry scrub and ghost trees of the jungle. A few minutes later, a jeep came careering through the dark blaring announcements in English and several other languages that I couldn't quite make out. There was to be a market day in Maravil. Everyone in the area was allowed to go on the morning bus. I could hardly believe it: a chance to go into the city where Uva had friends. A chance to find out if she, at least, had managed to get away. All evening I watched small deformed geckos twitch their plasma tails to the beat of crippled, brainless gnats hoping, like them, for a change in tempo.

I was up before the whistle blew the next morning. I had time to prepare – to squat, to rinse, to breakfast on stale bread – before setting out.

On the way to the main road, I caught sight of two buffaloes. One was trying to mount the other. The cow stumbled and the two beasts crashed into the trees. Then, behind the animals, a troop of soldiers appeared, jeering. They fired a few shots into the huddle. The male keeled over and the cow bolted, ripping the skin of her belly.

I have never been one easily angered, but my blood began to rise. If I had a gun, I suppose I might have used it. Then I remembered my grandfather piously quoting a pundit of his youth, 'Violence can only condemn you to more violence.' I understood that, but in my head I also heard my dead father, Lee, retort, 'Sometimes doing nothing condemns you more.'

The soldiers fired again, and went after the cow.

★   ★   ★

The bus appeared as a small yellow shimmering glob shaking itself out of a mirage pool. At the checkpoint a soldier ran a stick instrument under the vehicle. After he completed the inspection, one of his colleagues got on and the bus shuddered forward to the loading point. I was the only person waiting; my neighbours were at their own stop. The soldier checked me and allowed me to climb in.

Small fluorescent dots flashed on a screen by the steering wheel. The driver took no notice. He shoved another cud into his mouth and revved the engine. That morning there were no signs of any provisions. Only a few silent, weary people glued to rough vinyl benches. I sat by a window which had been smeared with oil and dust and stared out as if to carve my own route through the hot air.

A solitary drongo dropped from the sky and settled on the road ahead, its Y-tail sweeping a small arc in the dust. From Uva I thought, trying hard to contain my excitement. A messenger like the swallows I used to watch in my childhood; couriers from afar who had seemed to bear on each feather a signal for me from my absent father. It waited, without a sound, and took off when we began to move.

After picking up more silent passengers at the next stop, we rumbled down through a grove of stripped jacaranda trees and, eventually, reached an iron bridge built over a river of slow-moving green goo. The geometric shapes of the metal girders and the slabs of rock and mud were like the images in the glossy, chromatic photos I used to slip out of my father's envelopes as a child. He must have been here, I remember thinking, before this entire area degenerated.

On the other side of the river were the remains of an oil-palm plantation. I hadn't seen any before, but Uva had said that there were vast tracts of these inland. Each tree had been puffed to a regulation height before being allowed to wither either as a result of mismanagement, or by being junked as a project of an earlier regime.

I reckoned we travelled about twenty-five kilometres before reaching the coast where the plantation reverted back to coconut and lime. The sand was white with pulverised sea skeletons. There were white flecks in the sea too; small sodium pennants gathering together to rush the shore.

We came to a lagoon and I felt a hint of the optimism of my sea-crossing seep back into me. Uva had told me about a lagoon. Wrinkling up her face in distaste, she had explained that between the hotel and Maravil was a lagoon with a factory fish farm. Despite her disapproval, I felt a little less lost; but when I breathed in, the stink of prawns simmering made me want to retch. The land ahead was bent into a finger that seemed to reach right into my throat.

A little later the bus took another turn. Ahead of us the white cupolas of Maravil rose out of the scrag. High above another drongo circled, crying for its mate.

Most of Maravil had been built quickly after the older cities of the province had been destroyed. Therefore the main buildings were all formed out of identical cheap concrete blocks. The only distinguishing feature I could see were the domed roofs that a few of the taller ones had. According to Uva, the market square and the underground mall, originally a tourist project, were all that remained of the old town.

The bus slowed down. There were several vehicles on the road: we passed a lorry full of onions, a motor-cart heaped with coconuts, a sweaty refrigerated prawn truck, all gibbering towards the centre.

At a massive monument of a soldier, the bus turned left and ran alongside a canal until it reached the depot. About half a dozen other run-down buses had been crammed in, and more people than I had ever seen on the island. I climbed down from the bus and went over to a display board: a simplified map of the city and its surroundings with large areas to the north and the south blanked out. The canal and the market hall were outlined in red. I worked out our route. The compound, I figured, was in the shaded circle at the eastern end of the road. The Palm Beach Hotel and the village, therefore, had to be one of the settlements in the green stretch north of the lagoon. I stepped back to take in more of the map at a glance.

'You need pass?' A small, plump man peered from behind the board. 'Night pass, valid sundown-sunup. For Carnival Mall.'

I remembered Uva explaining that the mall was where her Jaz worked. 'Let's see?' I asked the tout.

The man's mouth shifted into a crude hook. 'Come, now.'

'What?'

'Come.' The man pulled out a round metal clam and prised it open. He checked the time. 'You do for me my asking for this much.' He indicated the passing of an illicit hour.

'Do what?'

'First agree.'

I shook my head, even though I was tempted.

'No hard work,' the man leered. 'Only pig stick.'

I didn't know what he meant. All I could think of was the barbaric pastime where hunters on horseback stuck spears into squealing hogs. I couldn't see this man doing that.

'Maybe later,' I said.

The little man's nose twitched as the wind broke behind him. 'Later may be too late. Passes go fast. This be the rub-rub night. But do what you like. No problem for me.'

I felt a small flutter of uncertainty inside, but I crushed it and moved on.

I could hear the market before I reached it. A low drone of electricity and the flapping of tarpaulins punctuated by the occasional sharp cry of a hawker. The street that led down to it was strewn with garbage and litter. A Roman arch framed the entrance and there was a soldier on duty outside it. He watched me pass through without stopping me.

The square inside was lined with small handcarts selling dubious-looking snacks and beverages: burnt gram, yeasty juices, dried molasses, wrinkled sausage sticks. Throngs of dishevelled people mooched about, looking rather than buying. The first vendor I passed sparked out of his mouth, 'Fizz, fizz, fizz.' Others near him then began to ululate softly, swaying from side to side. They looked as malnourished as the people milling around, especially compared to the young soldiers stationed on the steps.

The main hall was a type of structure I recognised from Eldon's history books, favoured in the past for recurrent displays of collective hubris: a large rectangular plinth with a series of columns supporting an angular roof. Under it, the area seemed to be divided into blocks. I could see vegetable stalls in the first row. Flesh, I noticed, was sold in a separate shed, where I supposed the smell of blood would not cloud the minds of the new recruits patrolling outside.

An old woman tipped a wicker basket containing a couple of deformed moon radishes towards me and waved her fingers in the air. 'Two one, two one.' Her loose breasts wobbled perilously in a cradle of dirty lace. Her face was streaked with a bitter, dark stain. I ignored her. I wanted information, not vegetables: something to help me find Uva, or her friends, or a consul.

Skirting a scattering of blemished aubergines and a few convoluted runner beans, I headed for the centre of the hall. There was no fruit anywhere to be seen. I remembered how Uva had explained to me that the authorities stipulated what could be grown and at what price it could be sold. She could not, however, explain to me why they didn't allow fruit. Why were her fruits and eggs and birds such a threat? When I said it made no sense to me she replied, 'Sense is not what they are about.'

The layout inside the hall was familiar. Markets have not changed, Eldon liked to say, in three thousand years; not in design, purpose or ethics.

Right in the middle I found a stall with a sign in English: Zengporium. An owlish man wearing spectacles was serving two elderly men. Uva had spoken about a trader called Zeng, but I couldn't be sure this was the same man. I took my time and sauntered up to the counter, hoping to hear something. The transaction was completed with hardly a word and the two customers shuffled away. The trader seemed very cool. I examined the small cellophane packets of arrowroot he had in front and then decided to take a chance. 'Uva says you have passes for the Carnival.'

He didn't move a muscle.

'Do you?'

His face contracted a little. 'Where'd she go?'

I figured there was nothing to lose by then. 'She disappeared about ten days ago,' I explained. 'I'm trying to find her.'

He inspected me over the tops of his spectacles. Then, with a loud exhalation, he pulled out a tin of spice grits and slid it across the counter. 'Meet me at the fountain plaza just iffore sundown.'

'Where?'

'By the Victory monument. The stone soldier, you know?'

I picked up the can and nodded, 'OK.' I mentally ticked another box, but I still wasn't sure how much I could trust him.

Zeng withdrew and I decided to look over the rest of the hall. I wanted to find out if anyone sold instruments, implements or utensils. Survival tools.

In the far corner of the hall, overlooking the canal, I came across a display of shields, lamps, cups, plates – all made of metal – and a selection of knives including what looked like a switchblade. I was surprised. Everything else looked strictly utilitarian. The copperware, though, was very elegantly done: sophisticated designs, careful workmanship. Each piece was flawless; each seam perfect and straight. Behind the counter a young man was decorating a brass tray with an intricate pattern of geese circling the moon.

'That's beautiful,' I said. I wanted to compliment the artisan. He was the first person I had come across since I arrived, besides Uva, who seemed to do anything with passion: an inner intensity.

He bowed his head of bushy, frazzled hair.

'You learn to do this here?'

He took a long noisy breath. His lips squirmed as though he was trying to find the right word to spit out.

'I mean, in this city?'

I could see he understood me, but he gave up on the word he was struggling to find and set to work on a sheet of metal instead. Placing it in a vice clamped on to a worktable, he folded the sheet over and smoothed down the edge with a wooden block. He then reversed it and put the other edge in to create a mirror groove. After smoothing that down too, he took the sheet of metal out and hooked one curled edge to the other to form a cylinder. He slid the shining copper cylinder over an iron mould so that the locked edges were held in place on top. Pulling out a small hammer from a shelf underneath, he proceeded to hammer down the seam to seal and harden it. I was fascinated by the deftness with which he transformed a flat sheet into a polished three-dimensional vessel. When he finished, he placed the piece next to the others and ran his fingers against them, tinkling them like the tubes of a wind chime. Then he pulled out the tray of knives and placed it on the worktop in front of me.

While I toyed with the switchblade, he pulled out a pair of familiar metal-capped ebony sticks from his pocket and flicked them apart. Carefully he placed the butterfly knife on his outstretched finger; the split hilt on one side and the blade on the other. It floated in the air, perfectly balanced. He lifted it up and the knife levitated, drawing him to his feet after it. A moment later he threw it, up in the air, and caught it by the handle. He then twirled it back into its sheath. Although he seemed tense and tongue-tied, I could see this was someone whose knife might easily have pricked more than one heart.

But was it hers? Or was it a copy?

'You made that too?'

The young man's head moved back.

I did not want to think of her captured, although it was impossible not to. Perhaps he was another friend. 'What's your name?' I asked.

'Kris.'

She'd never mentioned him. I looked around. I could see a flight of steps leading down to a paved parapet of concrete humps overlooking the canal. The water was thick with rubbish. A couple of soldiers were standing on the other side. I felt I had to have the butterfly blade. I turned back and threw ten of my tokens on to the counter. 'For *that* knife.'

'No.' Kris pushed them back at me. 'Mine is not for sale.'

On our last night together in the hotel, Uva had used her knife to whittle the bone of a sweetsop into a nautch-knot, a serpent's coil. When she finished, she spun the handle, bringing the two parts together, and said, 'Only by coming together can the blade be closed.'

I feared for her safety, separated from her weapon. I tried to visualise it and, in the end, decided the knife I had seen was not the same one. It was a close match, but I hadn't seen the ankh on it: the looped cross, the symbol of eternal life, her gender and our most important first metal.

Across the city sunlight intensified, bouncing off one white building after another. Even the oily water of the canal seemed to seethe in the heat.

The midday whistle blew twice; the metalworker quickly shut up his stall and headed towards the cafeteria where I could see some people assembling. I followed him, anxious but uncertain whether I should ask him about Uva. I stepped between a mat strewn with dried reptiles and a collection of battered, broken flashlights. The next moment, I lost sight of him. He had vanished.

I was hungry and joined a queue of men in overalls who seemed to be the only people able to afford a meal. I handed over the tokens required and was given a clump of overcooked brown seaweed and fried rubber rings.

Although there were about fifteen other people in the cafeteria with their tin bowls, hardly a word was spoken above the slurp and splutter of soporific feeding. The whole place was in a stupor. Even the flies had slowed down and toppled from one rim to another like drunks in a daze. The hot air around me and the warm blubber made me drowsy. If only Uva had been more careful, I remember thinking then . . . If only I had been too.

When they began to close up the cafeteria, I decided to take one more look around the market before the stalls were taken down. I couldn't find Kris again, nor Zeng. There was nothing more to help me. In the end I bought a cucumber and a cabbage to supplement my diet at the compound, and a small string bag to carry them in.

There was still quite a bit of time, I reckoned, before I was due to meet Zeng. The bus back to the compound was meant to leave soon after the final whistle heralded the shrouding of the city. I wasn't sure how I was going to manage. I'd have to collect the pass, and then run back to the depot to catch the bus. Then I'd have to find a way of coming back . . . Of course I was being naïve; Zeng might not even turn up. I had to check out what else was possible.

I left the market by another gate and headed towards some bigger buildings, hoping some sign would lead me to the special enclave Uva had mentioned. I thought something might be possible there, despite her scepticism.

After about two hundred metres, I came to a security cordon. The soldiers looked hostile; they didn't speak but it was clear I was not allowed to go through. I tried a couple of other streets with similar results.

Eventually I found myself back at the bus depot. It was already quite empty; even the morning's tout had withdrawn. My options were closing fast. Straight ahead, the light in the sky was turning lurid as though blood was pumping out of a wound. A large tulip tree began to stir as small rodents prepared for nightfall.

I quickly retraced the route the bus took in the morning, along the canal, and found the monument and the fountain plaza. The monument was more complex than I had noticed from the bus. The stone military hero seemed to be celebrating a victory over several garuda-like warriors he had slain. It was out of their wounds that the fountain spurted.

Some real soldiers were taking a break, sipping beer with their guns half-cocked, on the benches. There was no sign of Zeng. I went and sat on the wall around a smaller fountain from where I could see the whole of the plaza, feeling quite spent.

'All ready?' Zeng nudged me.

'How did you get here?'

'You too tired. Dropping off, eh?'

My eyes hurt. 'No. I expected you along the canal road.'

'So, you want to visit the Carnival?'

'I am looking for Uva.'

'She's there?'

'You telling me, or asking me?'

'Asking, asking.'

'I don't know. Our plans got a little upset. But she mentioned one or two people ...' I hesitated, then gave the only other name I knew. 'Like Jaz?'

Zeng did not seem impressed. 'You know the Juice Bar?'

'Yes, of course.' I don't know why I lied. Panic, I suppose. Uva had told me so little.

Zeng studied me. Was he too looking for some sign of commitment? It was not the politics of the island that had brought me. I had come for something much more primal. I wondered whether he could understand that. I wanted him to trust me, but I didn't know how to show him that he could. I wished I hadn't lied.

His head moved slightly. Then he proceeded to explain that the Juice Bar had a blue lantern hanging outside it. Jaz, he said, was usually there. 'He is now the Pin manager.' He handed me a small laminated card. There was a metal barcode imprinted on it. Nothing else. 'You know how to use this?'

It was a familiar enough device but I had not come across any machines in Maravil that could use plastic cards. I rubbed the tag on my ear. 'I've been a little ... damaged.'

Zeng dipped a finger in the greasy water of the fountain and drew a wet map on the stone ledge. He showed me how to get to the Carnival checkpoint in the evaporating slime. 'You know it is underground. You must go straight to the metal box before the barrier. If there is a soldier there, don't talk. Just insert the card. Everything is automatic. As soon as it comes out, take it and walk through the steel door that will open. Do not lose the card. You will need it to come out again. It will work only this one night.' His lips tightened over the ridges of his teeth. 'I do this for her, OK? You better be careful.'

The box, luminous in the fast-failing light, whirred for ages before regurgitating the card. My whole body broke into a sweat. The soldier in his sentry-box was asleep. I should have been on the bus, going back. I didn't know how long I had before someone would come looking for me, but I had to go in. My only chance now was to find her Jaz. The door slowly cranked open. I covered the tiny metal hospital tag pinned to my ear and crept in.

Behind the door, a tunnel descended lit by a line of small round bulbs. Black dust frosted the top of each bulb and lay between the spiralling ribs of the concrete floor.

Expecting at any moment to be challenged, I followed the tunnel down, tripping from one sphere of light to the next. It looked to me more like the ramp of a car park than an exclusive entrance. I came to a swing door that led to the upper gallery of the underground mall: it could have been something built under a hotel or an office block anywhere in the world – thirty years ago. It was still unfinished, and looked like it always would be. Most of the units were bare; there were cables sticking out of the concrete in twisted loops at every corner. From where I stood I could see galleries on two floors, with a few shops selling clothes, and the main promenade sporting a bakery and a couple of cafés. These looked to me no more inviting than the cafeteria in the market, but the people who were drifting around looked in better shape. My clothes, I reckoned, would not set me apart too much among them. The only problem was that there was no sign of a bar and not even a flicker of blue among the tiers of dull lamps. Pressed against the cold galvanised railing, not sure what to do next, I felt stupid for believing Zeng. Stupid also for taking the risk, and stupid for thinking Uva would really have come anywhere near such a place. Stupid and more than a little scared.

'Fear is not cowardice,' Eldon had always maintained. 'To be brave, one must know fear and learn to overcome it. Release it, not instil it.' It was a theory I wanted to subscribe to. I took the stairs down to the promenade.

Only once I was down at that level did I glimpse the blue beacon, flickering beyond the empty atrium tubs. I hurried towards it, stooping so that my height would not be too noticeable.

When I finally reached the Juice Bar, I lingered outside. I remembered how Uva had spoken of Jaz as though he belonged to a profane underworld I could never bridge. But why not? If she could, why couldn't I?

Hiding my fists in my pockets, string bag swinging, I entered. Inside, scarab lamps burned in a dozen miniature alcoves. As my eyes adjusted, I made out a cluster of young men and women, preening and clucking. On a small mirrored stage, a troupe of nubile, genderless creatures with shaven bodies gyrated to the hard relentless noise of a dance machine. Two girls and a bleached boy detached themselves from the huddle and crowded around me. 'Happy . . . ?' the boy mewed through lips of gilt and glitter. I missed the other word as the drums intensified.

'Happy tea,' the high-booted girl echoed cuddling up. I held her at bay and shouted out Jaz's name, trying to raise my voice above the racket. The boy smiled knowingly and passed me a bowl of mist. I took a sip and felt, for an instant, that my head had come apart; the mouthful spread through me deadening each cell in my body, one by one, until my flesh unreeled from my bones. Someone struck a flint and flames streaked across the room lighting a river of spirits to burn what looked like spunk off the floor.

I asked for water, plain water.

'Try the bar,' the girl pouted and pushed me towards the back of the room. The deranged electrons around me had no rhythm, no anchor. I was spinning.

Then behind the bar, I spotted Jaz.

He was unmistakable. A radiant face, embellished by the glossy curved lips of a charmfish; dark eyes twinkling over a rococo amethyst necklace, and a bare body of thin light muscle enmeshed in the filigree chain-cloth of a silver waistcoat laced on each side. Around his middle he had a tiny pleated tangy-green sarong tied with a fantail bustle at the back. 'Speak up, darling.' He cupped a hand to his left ear, distinctly larger than his right, compensating the twist of his taut body as he leaned over, exposing a gleaming buttock and exuding the scent of cinnamon and honey. 'Into my ear, will you?' he coaxed.

'Are you Jaz?'

The machine music faded.

'And who are you, gorgeous?' Jaz fluttered his malachite lids luxuriously. He was younger than me, but knew exactly what he could do with his body.

I shook the echoes out of my head and looked around; I was sober again. I moved nearer. 'Uva said you were her friend.'

The mention of Uva made him straighten up in surprise. 'Oh, you must be the darling new lover then? Tall one, huh?'

I was relieved; she must have told him about me. 'Do you know where she is?'

'Marc, isn't it?' He reached across the bar. 'Nice hands. Very nice.'

'Do you?' I repeated. I was beginning to doubt that he could help me. 'Do you know what has happened?'

Jaz feigned an exaggerated concern. 'Why, you haven't already had a little tiff, have you?' He moved my hand gently aside and swatted a small red termite with a coaster. His arm, his bare hairless chest, his face all shone with what looked like serum. He seemed incapable of understanding the danger she might be in. I wondered whether he was really a friend, or just a kind of doll she liked to play with. How much could I safely say to him?

'They found her . . . place.' I tried to form the words into small, hard pellets in my mouth. 'She hasn't been here then? She hasn't told you?'

His ebullient face lost its shape. Jaz closed his eyes for a second; he began to breathe faster. His girlish breasts swelled and subsided within the flaps of his shimmering waistcoat. Then he looked again at my face. 'How did you get in here?' His voice dropped.

'A mutual friend.' Although there was no trace of suspicion in his question, I really could not be sure of him. I felt I couldn't trust anyone.

Jaz reached up to a shelf above and took down a pair of glasses. From behind he got a bottle of Pin and poured out two drinks. He slid one across. 'I think I need a drink.'

I picked up the glass warily. 'You have plain water?'

He rolled his eyes, but passed me a pitcher and another glass.

I poured myself some water. 'I've been in a compound. I thought she might have got in touch with you. She told me that you were the one who could get almost anything done here.'

'Such an exaggerator.' Jaz shrank back, turning coy. 'I

haven't seen her in ages. I just heard about you on the grapevine.'

I checked to see if he'd said that because somebody was listening in. There was nobody near us.

Jaz rested his face on his fingertips for a moment. Then he said quietly, 'If she has been taken in, the information will be posted on the official database.' A slight note of mischief pinked his voice again. 'There is a terminal I think I can access. Come with me.' Jaz strapped a pouch around him and slipped out from behind the bar. He snaked across the room to a young man standing with his face fixed on the emasculated dancers gathering back on stage. Jaz sidled up to him. 'Hi, you are the Warden's guest?'

The young man looked startled.

'Where is she?' he cooed.

'She's just gone to the salon . . .'

'First time in the Carnival? Your aura, you see. I knew it. Is it art you have come for? Or a bit of our serendipity . . . ?'

The young man shifted, embarrassed, and looked down at his feet.

'Oh, but I love the way you bite that zunge. Has anyone ever told you just how *sexy* that is?'

I was getting a little irritated and cleared my throat, but Jaz ignored my interruption.

'Oh, what a darling little thing.' He stroked the young man's placid hand and then hooked an arm around his waist, 'This is a wonderful spot for you. You'll love it here.' As he chatted Jaz fussed with his victim's wrists, collar, strip-line lapel and the plastic toggle of his zipper, opening and closing it to the buzz of the resumed dance music as though massaging the linings of his suit. The young man struggled at first, but seemed unable to release himself without slipping completely out of his jacket. I watched mortified as he finally succumbed.

Jaz then steered the young man to a chair and kissed him firmly on the lips. 'You'll have a fine time here. The juicers are simply divine, especially that ravishing bleach boy.' He tipped a spirit lamp into a ring of fire around the tightly crossed feet. 'Ciao, for now. You'll be really primed, darling, when the flames go down.'

Jaz turned to me. 'Let's go. We have to be quick.' He led the way, out through the back, into an unlit wasteway. 'He is the Warden's new boy.'

'Warden?'

'Although this is a leisure zone, there still has to be some authority: that's the Warden. She runs all the pleasure parlours here for the District Commander and has a terminal in her hut.' He showed me a silvery card, 'And we needed this from that boy to get in.'

'How did you know he'd have one?'

'I too was one of her favourites.' Jaz's teeth flashed in the dim glow of a paper moon pinned to the ceiling. 'A member of her inner circle. But she took away my card last time.'

'Why? What did you do?'

'*Nothing*, sweetie. That was the trouble. I knew she wanted to change her pleasure puck, so I was a little ungenerous. Withholding, you might say,' he sniggered. 'Let's go quickly. I feel kind of odd out here.'

Jaz's legs were bare. Thin and shaved. His feet were squeezed into gimcrack clogs that announced each step he took with a hollow clip and a clop. He went ahead, teetering, until we came to a separate unit painted black with several aerials sticking out at different heights. 'This is the hut.'

'Won't there be guards?'

'No. The card is the guard. We can get in. She'll be in the salon for ages before meeting up with the boy, and he will be completely out of his head, poor thing.'

Using the stolen card, Jaz let us in. The reception room was bare. There were paper-screen doors on two of the walls. Jaz knew which to open and took me down a hall to a large office. He went straight to a chunky computer console that looked like it belonged in a museum. He quickly donned a small headset. 'This must be one that still uses passwords,' I said.

Jaz grinned. 'Yep. She's a lazy cow. She never changes them.' He activated the screen with his fingers.

Watching him log on, I thought this couldn't possibly work. Even such old junk must have some built-in security. I was wrong. A couple of anxious minutes later Jaz had located the prison gazette. The knot in my stomach tightened. He searched for her name. Nothing came up. He flitted from one icon to another. 'No sign of her,' he said. He had reached the exit-box. Then he checked the news items. 'Nothing.'

'Is there a command site?' I asked. 'Can we check who they are hunting?'

'Hunting is all they ever do, my dear. They hunt everything here.'

He whizzed in and out of screens until he found a page of index photos. 'These are the ones in purgatory. Maybe they put her in a camp like yours.' Jaz simpered and zoomed in. It was my mugshot fixed against a red background. The caption gave the information about my capture and suspected involvement with a subversive. Underneath my number – 1661 – was a link to another page. 'Maybe that link is the one we want.' He clicked on it. I shut my eyes: green, green, let the background be green. When I opened my eyes I saw her: her face sucked in, one eye half-closed, her hair tied into a flare against a pea-green background. The information was that she had been last seen at the Palm Beach Hotel. 'That is a really old photo,' Jaz laughed and turned around. 'Your little angel is still free.' I put my hands on his back, too grateful to think. Then he hit the reverse button. 'Now with this one,' he tut-tutted, 'they should have taken a three-quarter shot and caught that little cheekbone of yours, at least.'

Seconds after he spoke I heard a screen-door open. Jaz's hands froze. I heard a squeak in the hall. I pressed the cancel button in front of Jaz and slipped off my stool, down behind a tall metal cabinet. A moment later two burly security guards peeped into the room. Looking through the steel mesh between the shelves, I could see they were combat-trained: they wore cat's eye helmets, unlike Nirali at the hotel, and gripped their automatic weapons firmly, with both hands. One of them greeted Jaz by his name. Neither seemed surprised to find him there. But Jaz was clearly rattled. He pulled off his headphones and asked how they got in.

'The door was open. We knew she wasn't here, and thought we better look. So you are back in now?'

'Waiting, you know . . .' He managed a salacious grin.

I tried not even to breathe. It might have been better if I hadn't hidden; we could have bluffed our way out. One of the guards stepped a little closer and glanced at the console in front of Jaz.

'How *do* you get the movie channel?' Jaz's voice jumped an octave. 'Do you guys know how to do that?'

The guard twiddled a knob and ran his hand over the buttons. The other guard paced around the room, his boots creaking as if about to split with his ponderous weight.

My heart was a steel drum. I wished I could muffle it.

Jaz started gabbling again, nervously pulling at the hem of his mini sarong. 'Do you know when the Warden is coming back? I thought she was going to be here. She told me to come . . .'

The guard next to him tapped another button on the console and the screen sprang into life. Uva's face stared out. The guard stared back. The second guard shunted over and craned his neck to look.

'Why is *she* there?' Jaz's voice rose in astonishment. 'What's it mean?' He rushed the words too fast.

The guards studied him but didn't say anything. The first one picked up a headset and put it on. The picture shifted. There was information there about Uva and the fact that she was wanted. He scratched his chin listening; the other one was beginning to look impatient. His face twisted as he tried to understand what might be going on. Jaz gripped the edge of the desk to stop his hand from shaking. When the data flow stopped the guard put down the headset and stared at Jaz. 'Where?' he growled.

'What?'

'Where is she?'

'She hasn't come down here for ages. I haven't seen her.'

'Why are you looking then?'

Jaz fidgeted about. 'I . . .' he faltered. 'I was just messing about and . . .'

The other guard stomped over. 'Searching, no?'

Jaz sucked in his big lips. 'Look, I was looking for some pictures. The Warden showed me before, but I couldn't work out . . .'

71

The smaller guard pulled his communicator out of its holster and pressed a button. The other man watched him. 'Warden's not answering,' the one with the communicator grumbled.

As he clicked another button, I realised that it was up to me to somehow disarm them. I rocked back, tensing my muscles. I held my breath, and then shoved the cabinet at the two guards. It crashed into them and sent them sprawling on the floor. I scrambled out, grabbed one of their fallen guns and pointed it at the heaving flab. The gun was much heavier than Nirali's; I had to step back a couple of paces to keep my balance. 'Shoot, shoot,' Jaz hissed. I hesitated. My finger was on the trigger, but the cat's eye in the centre of the nearest soldier's forehead stopped me. I heard Eldon scolding my father for becoming an air warrior, for wanting to bury a bullet in someone's brain.

Rope, rope, I needed rope and their surrender. Then there was an explosion as the other guard snatched back a gun and fired. Half a dozen bullets riddled the ceiling. A siren went off outside.

I yanked Jaz by the arm and we took off. 'You should have got them while you could,' he whined. I banged the door behind me and we ran down to the corner and hid in a doorway.

On the main promenade people had gathered together, frightened by the siren.

'What happens with this alarm?' I asked Jaz.

'I don't know. It hasn't happened before.' The mascara around his eye had spread like a bruise.

I saw the two soldiers stumbling out of the hut and further down another bunch of soldiers descending a stairway. 'More.' Jaz crouched low. The numbers of civilians on the promenade began to swell as the rattle of boots grew. 'What can we do?'

I was trying to get my bearings when I saw a woman break away from the crowd and nip into the alleyway opposite us. She had one of Jaz's bar bottles in her hand and was stuffing it with a piece of cloth. Jaz saw her too. 'She's crazy. We must stop her.' I held him back; the soldiers would have seen him if he tried to cross over. I watched in a sort of paralysis as she set fire to the cloth and then, darting out, hurled it at the squad of soldiers in the centre. The bottle burst into flames. The soldiers scattered, firing in the direction from which the missile had been launched. 'Fire, fire, fire,' the woman chanted. Another volley of shots echoed in the mall. People screamed; several in the crowd fell, writhing as if skewered. One man, clutching his head, lurched towards the soldiers pleading; others scrambled to the upper floors and flung more bottles and stools, pipes and glass, from the galleries and stairways. Within moments the whole area was in mayhem.

Was that woman, like Uva, another subversive? 'She a friend?' I asked Jaz.

He shook his head. 'She's a nutter. She's had too much. We have got to get out.' His whole body sagged; his eyes were squeezed small in his face as if he didn't want to see what was happening.

'But is Uva with her?' I grabbed him and forced him to listen to me.

'No, I tell you. She is not in here. I am sure of it.'

'Come with me, then. This way.' I pulled him towards the stairs I had come down earlier. 'You'll have to run.'

Jaz clutched hold of me with both hands, 'Where?'

We climbed up to the top floor where I had first emerged from the tunnel. From there I looked back and saw smoke pour out of one of the cafés. There was another blaze further down, near the Juice Bar. I couldn't work out whether this was a spontaneous uprising, or something planned. 'How is it possible?' I asked Jaz. 'I thought the people down here were all zombies.'

Jaz stopped. 'Did you?' His eyes hardened, briefly.

I didn't understand then how close we all live to the brink. 'Look, we better get out this way.' I pushed ahead into the tunnel.

When I reached the exit machine, I rammed Zeng's card in. It disappeared but nothing happened.

Jaz hobbled up behind me.

I asked him for his pass.

'They would have blocked all of them by now.'

I tried it anyway. Still nothing happened. Jaz squatted down and hugged his knees. 'What are we gonna do?'

The door was made of steel.

I ran my fingers quickly along the edges of the exit machine. 'There must be an emergency bypass.'

'What bypass? Why should there be any bypass?' Jaz buried his head in his arms.

'Because that is the way things are made. Everything has an emergency bypass.' Right at the bottom I located a small screw. 'There. See?' I used the rolled edge of a token to unscrew it. It turned easily, but when it came out there was nothing but an empty hole there.

'Now what?'

I stood up. There was only one thing to do. Cocking the gun, I put the muzzle into the metal slit and fired. This I could do then. I could pull the trigger if the target didn't breathe. There was a terrific squawk of surprised electronics and the steel door opened.

★   ★   ★

74

Outside, the sentry-box was empty. Jaz touched my arm. 'Where are they?' he asked half-covering his mouth with his other hand.

'They must have all gone down.'

'What do we do?'

I found it impossible to think clearly. 'You are sure she couldn't be down there too.'

'Absolutely.'

'What about up here? Could she be hiding somewhere else in the city?'

Jaz put both his hands on me and drew in his breath. 'I don't know how I can say this, but you are the one who must calm down now.' He waited a moment. 'You spoke to a friend of hers up here? Was it Zeng? What did he say?'

'He didn't even know they were after her.'

Jaz released my arm. 'Then she's way out somewhere. He would know if she was anywhere in the city.'

I thought we should be running. The soldiers would be coming after us. But I couldn't move. I felt something was settling into place between us. Trust? Something more? 'We better get out of this town too. I know where she will be heading. Across the cordon, over the hills . . . to Samandia.' I looked at Jaz: he seemed small and delicate in the open air. 'You'd better come with me. They'll know you had a hand in all that down there.'

Jaz's face turned ashen. 'Into the jungle?'

'Only if we get that far,' I snapped.

'I've always been a city duck, you know. Chittagong would suit me better.'

I put up my hand. 'OK, OK, whatever. Just tell me, how do we get out of here first?'

Jaz hesitated. The moisture in his eyes caught a distant

light as he glanced quickly around. 'Maybe if we go to the warren someone will help us. It's down the hill.'

That was the general direction from which I had come; I set off, walking briskly. Jaz removed his clogs and trotted anxiously behind.

Near the bottom of the hill he caught up and pointed out a street leading to some ramshackle workshops. 'Through there.'

Several of the workshops had white flowluxes on. A few tired men were tinkering with boxes and machinery unaware of the pandemonium raging underground. One or two looked up as Jaz in his flamboyant costume flitted across their doorways, but they did not show any interest.

'Do you know anyone here?' I asked Jaz.

He plucked at his lips and shook his head. 'No, but I know Uva does.'

At the far end of the lane, I saw a krypton beam pierce the outer darkness and then search out a wall, a window, a door. I heard barking. I couldn't tell if the dogs were coming closer or not. Then a flowlux at the end of the street lit up three soldiers with guns in their hands. They were walking slowly, stopping at every doorway. I held Jaz back. My mouth was dry. My tongue slid back down my gullet. Jaz wriggled, his skin slippery. I tried to grip him hard but I was afraid I might crack a bone. Through a window I recognised the coppersmith from the market – Kris. Deciding to risk it, I led Jaz into the workshop. Kris looked up surprised.

'We have to hide.' I had to trust my intuition.

He stared at the gun in my hand.

We heard a vehicle coming down the lane. It stopped outside the workshop. The engine was left throbbing. I thought they must have followed us. I raised the gun. We could hear the voices of soldiers alighting, orders, boots. I looked at Kris but he avoided my eyes. 'They are after us,' I hissed. We heard the soldiers go next door. I couldn't tell how many. Kris was listening too. Then he seemed to come to a decision. He indicated a storeroom at the back and I hustled Jaz into it.

'Who is he?' Jaz whispered, putting his head against mine.

I closed the door. 'A metalworker, Kris, from the market.' I didn't mention the butterfly knife I had seen. If he wasn't a friend, then he'd be a betrayer. I looked around for a way to escape. Jaz watched me.

The soldiers clattered into the workshop. I heard a grunt. A slap and the crash of something toppling. One of the soldiers swore. Then there was the thud of flesh being hit. Another crash. Peeping through a crack in the wood, I saw Kris on the ground staring at the shattered struts of the piece he had been working on. A table, behind him, had also collapsed; his tools and his hoard of metal strips were everywhere. I remember feeling guilty for doubting him. Two soldiers gloated over the mess. One had a stick which he used like a bat to hit a ball of wire. The other went up to Kris and kicked him. Kris doubled up and the soldier kicked him again. I had a gun and there were only two soldiers in the room. I could stop them. There'd be a fighting chance with the rest. A voice called out from across the road. The first soldier went out to investigate while the one who kicked Kris saw our door and started towards it. I eased the safety catch off the gun and tried to still my hand. Then I saw Kris rise, the butterfly knife open in his fist. A moment later he had his arm around the soldier's throat. I shut my eyes, nausea already in my mouth as though the knife behind the soldier's back was penetrating my own body. When I looked again the soldier was a crumpled heap on the floor. Kris was standing, sombre and straight, with the soldier's gun in his hand.

Jaz rushed over to Kris. 'You killed him?'

Kris's face was set hard, his head slightly bowed.

Jaz turned to me, panic filling his eyes. 'He's dead.' Jaz looked as though he didn't understand what he was saying. Perhaps he had never seen a dead man close up.

The blood on the floor was bright. I saw my grandfather with a flower bleeding in his hand. My world seemed to be fracturing faster than ever. For years I had tried to keep it still, undisturbed, despite the shocks I've had to endure. Love, Uva promised, would make it strong; now it seemed she was wrong. I remembered how she spoke of life always springing out of death. The idea filled me more with foreboding than comfort. Death was not what I had come looking for.

'How can we get out of here?' My throat was clogged. I found it hard to speak.

'There's the cruiser outside,' Kris suggested quietly, still looking down. 'I could show you the way to the hills.'

Avoiding the body, I edged along the wall to the window. A sleek military land-cruiser was idling empty in the lane, the headlights on. Voices were raised in a building further down.

'OK, let's go.' I grabbed hold of Jaz, and shepherded him up to the vehicle. Kris should have been behind me, watching out; instead he stayed behind to collect some things in a holdall. I bundled Jaz into the back seat and tried to beckon Kris. He took no notice and continued packing. Then, after a quick last look, he zipped the bag and clicked a switch. It was only then that I remembered my string bag from the market. I'd left it in Jaz's bar.

'You drive.' Kris looked as if something was caged inside

78

him. He shifted the gun from one hand to the other. I slipped behind the wheel. I checked the controls; they were quite conventional, but when I touched the panel lights, the steady throb of the engine dropped slightly. I was terrified it would stall. Kris stood on the footboard and kept the sliding door open. 'Go right down to the end and turn left. If they come out, charge them. I'll use this.' He lifted up his gun.

I released the brake and the vehicle rolled forward.

Halfway down the cracked alleyway, a puzzled soldier stepped out into the beam of the cruiser's headlights. He shaded his eyes with one hand and waved his gun about. I saw Kris had his levelled. He was squinting. 'Don't shoot, he'll jump out of the way.' I gunned the engine. But as the vehicle surged forward, the soldier stiffened his grip and fired. The shots fractured the upper windscreen into a profusion of silver webs before Kris's burst of bullets hit him. I hunkered down and jammed the accelerator to the floor: the cruiser flew. *A wing and a prayer*, a phrase Eldon claimed was meant for angels not airmen, however much they might wish it, sailed through my mind. I dipped my lights, thankful that the force of Kris's bullets had hurled the soldier out of my path. At the end of the alley I spun the wheel and the cruiser bumped over the painted kerb on to the main road. I checked with Kris, who merely nodded.

There was nobody else on the road. A rush of reckless hope shot from the ball of my foot, pressing on the accelerator, right up to my head. I drove fast. I had never driven like that before. Speed was a salve then: exhilaration replacing the terror that had been growing in me before. Within minutes we had left the city behind. The road curved ahead and Kris warned of a roadblock after the next turn.

'Roadblock?' Jaz gasped behind me.

'The road to the hills is on the right soon after,' Kris replied.

'What about this roadblock?'

'You just hold tight back there.' I kicked down into a lower gear and accelerated.

Jaz flopped back and grabbed the grip-bar; Kris braced himself with his foot against the kit-box.

I took the turn at high speed and swung the cruiser around the oil drums in a slalom. The tyres squealed. The tailcage banged into one drum sending it reeling across the road. I rammed the rest and we burst through the barrier. The solitary soldier in the pill-box opened fire but, with a cool snipe-swerve, we flew out of range. Jaz gave a whoop of delight, clapping hysterically. 'Go, Marc, go.' Even Kris seemed to breathe a little easier pressed against the seatback, his gun clamped between his knees.

Outside the boundaries of Maravil, the headlights cut the night wide open. 'Is this the right turn?' I asked.

'Yes,' Kris nodded. 'Yes.'

The road was rough but straight. There were no planta-tions, no houses, no huts that I could see. Plain scrubland, I guessed. As time passed, my muscles slowly relaxed. I had been gripping the steering wheel hard; my shoulders were stiff. I let them drop. I felt heavier. The cruiser felt heavier. I slowed down; there was no sign of anyone chasing us. I was tired. I didn't know how long I had been driving but we had travelled a good enough distance. I wanted to let go. I wanted to rest. Jaz's head lolled on the top edge of my seat. I felt his sleepy breath like a warm tide lapping, a soft hand fingering the nape of my neck; stroking, soothing, comforting.

★   ★   ★

Uva's breath was never like that; it always seemed so much my own. Even now I do not believe it is possible for it to cease without my life ending. It cannot. And yet, sometimes she seems to fade like our memories of wings.

'You think there are mermaids of the air?' she asked me once, as we listened to the warplanes patrol the brief electrified twilight of the Palm Beach coast. 'Some creatures that know more than us, that can save us from damaging our poor sky staring so sadly into space?'

'Why sadly?'

'Don't you think the clouds are full of tears? Whose could they be?'

I unfastened the sleeves of her tunic. 'Your little garuda's? Or an angel's?' I pinched the line from Eldon tipping his hat at a cloud bringing rain to a parched summer's day. 'The sky is crying,' I remembered him saying, 'another angel has lost its wings.'

Later, when the road finally split into two, I turned again to Kris. 'Which way?'

His head listed to one side as though he had to listen to the magnetic thrum of some inner needle. He then flicked his hand upwards suggesting the track that climbed up the small slope. It led us to the top of a bund containing a vast nebulous expanse that seemed to disappear in the distance. I stopped the cruiser on the ridge.

'Go around the lake, we will soon reach the hills.'

'No more roadblocks?' My mind's map of the island was still incomplete, but I knew we must be in the middle north. The scrub jungle around Uva's parents' unsurrendered hope: the last wild gene pool in the central mountains.

'They only have those in the cordons around the cities and camps.'

I closed my eyes and tried to imagine what I could not see.

Kris opened the door and jumped out. He went down to the water.

'Be careful,' I called out. 'It may be contaminated.'

Jaz, behind me, cleared his throat. 'I'm thirsty. We don't have anything to drink.' He reached out and touched my elbow. 'Can't we drink it?'

'I wouldn't.' The grey pall above the surface was like the sick air that clung to the waterhole near my concrete compound.

The wind picked up and the water began to swell and break. The moonlight retracted into small smears, stars became smudged.

Kris climbed back in and I started the engine. We moved along the bund, slowly, buffeted by gusts of wind.

Then the sky was ripped white. The vehicle seemed to explode. Jaz shrieked. Another searing flash and eruption followed. I raced the engine. After I got over the initial shock, I felt like shouting for more. This was nature. I could contend with it. Outside, bolt after bolt of lightning fused the earth, melting its contours.

'What's that roar? What is it?' Jaz tugged at my sleeve, terrified.

A phalanx of molten spears engulfed us as the rain hit the vehicle, ploughing the earth bund and churning the waters of the tank.

'Rain,' Kris bellowed. 'It's only rain.'

I had never driven in rain like that. I was sure the bund would disintegrate and we'd go into the lake. I turned off and drove down away from it, between large granite boulders that I could just about see. On the flat we came to a broken enclosure of a colossal rock. I stopped the vehicle. 'There's a cave,' Jaz hollered. The downpour seemed to double; the pounding on the roof was deafening. I picked up a flashlight. Kris clipped another flashlight to his belt, next to his knife, and picked up his gun.

I led the way, sprinting.

Inside was dry, and the roar at least was not right in our ears. I shone the torch around the cave: there were remains of walls, stone plinths and neatly cut shelves. While I looked around, uncertain as to what to do next, Kris stripped off his clothes. 'Hey,' Jaz started, wide-eyed, as Kris swung, naked, back into the rain. 'Is he having a wash now?' Jaz's voice rose to the light, irrepressible falsetto he liked to play with.

When Kris reappeared he had a small plastic bottle of rainwater, and a sponge. He handed the bottle to Jaz, and then stepped aside to wipe himself with the sponge.

I pointed the light at it. 'This you can drink,' I said to Jaz.

He swallowed the rainwater in big noisy gulps. Then he went over to Kris and took the sponge from him. 'Thank you, Kris,' he said drying his back for him, tenderly.

The cave was large and had clearly been made into some sort of a temple. It felt safe, perhaps because it offered us shelter. Sitting there though, despite the dark, I felt there was something more to it. Something more benign.

When the rain finally eased, we collected the seat-pads from the cruiser, and some coverings, and brought them into the cave. I sat up on a ledge, watching over the other two, as they settled in a huddle like children.

I was exhausted but my body would not unwind. I remember thinking one of us ought to stay up on guard, even though I wasn't sure what good it would do. I stared out as though by looking I could make Uva appear. I wanted to pray for her and wished I knew how. I wish I knew now, remembering.

The air seemed to cool as the storm moved further away. I reached over and adjusted the blanket that had slipped off Jaz's bare round shoulder. He was sound asleep.

III

MOON PLAINS

I WOKE up remembering my grandfather crying. It was the last spring before the years of our evergrowing shadows, more unsettled than anyone had expected.

On that late May day, in the gardens along the Thames, everybody's roses were in bloom. The sun was bright, but the sky hazy and the roar of jet planes coming in to land seemed louder for their invisibility. I was spending a few days with my grandparents while my mother was away at one of her innumerable conferences. Blackbirds were chi-chi-ing incessantly and the maroon roses on the straggly branches, too high up the neighbour's wall for my grandfather to reach, blossomed where the sun had warmed the buds into heavy blooms with ball gown pleats and voluminous petals. My grandfather was resting on his rustic oak bench, feasting his eyes on the butterfly florescence of a deliciously yellow laburnum tree. It was mid-afternoon. The garden was a riot of colour. Eldon, nearly eighty years old, seemed completely at peace.

'Granda, are you going?' I asked.

'Where?'

'To the show.'

He had been looking at a newspaper article on the Chelsea

flower show. 'I don't think so. It's not for people like me. Anyway, the crowds will tire me out.' He sighed, as he often did, and lit another cigarette. He turned the page to the cricket which was his other restorative. His team – the old home team – was on a roll.

'You want to play with the hosepipe?' He pointed a crumpled cigarette at a spool of green plastic tubing by the fence. 'Those roses need water.' His tone suggested that the sight of the spray would revive him too: a gushing pipe in warm, still air. 'Pull it out.'

On my way over, I spotted a mound of crumbly brown earth at the border of the lawn. I plucked a dandelion and poked at it with the furry stem.

'What have you found?' Eldon called out. 'Don't you want the hose?'

I reluctantly left the colony of alarmed ants and got hold of the pipe.

'Turn the tap on,' he instructed from his resting place. 'There is a control on the nozzle.'

The tap squeaked in my hand and bubbled. Stepping over a line of seedling cabbage, I unwound the hosepipe. A dribble from where the crosshatched plastic was locked into the red ring wet my feet. 'It's coming, Granda,' I shouted holding down the trigger with both hands and tracing a silver line to the edge of his oval lawn. Water poured into the dry earth of the flower bed like a river. A muddy puddle quickly formed and a rich gurgle filled the garden.

'Turn it some more so you get a proper spray.'

I wanted to run the water to the ants. A little trench quickly filled; a dark foaming head slithered towards the nest.

'Do the roses, Marc. The roses. Give each bush a good

minute and a half. Count to a hundred, then move to the next.'

All of a sudden my arms went limp. I wanted to cry. 'Granda, do ants drown?'

For a moment he looked blank, as though he was trying to work out whether ants breathed. Whether they had noses and nostrils. Lungs that might fill with water. Whether their tiny legs would flail, splashing about, before they sank down beneath the surface. He gazed at me as though I was somebody else. 'Yes, son. Yes, I suppose they do.'

'Have you ever killed an ant, Granda?' I wanted his hand to give mine the strength I could not find.

'You mean deliberately?' He hunched his shoulders as though he was in a fighter plane, like my father, swooping down, with the gun muzzles on the wing blades jabbering neat lines of dust-puffs to match the spasms of a dying column. 'I never flew even the Hurricanes,' he muttered.

I didn't understand. 'What hurry cranes?' I asked.

'I mean not into combat,' he added absently. 'But what did you ask?'

'If you ever killed an ant.'

'No, never. Never deliberately.'

I was wondering about accidents when Grandma Cleo called out, 'Eldon, telephone.'

He heard her, but it took him some time to return from his reverie.

'Eldon, telephone for you.'

'Right.'

I watched him stub his cigarette out on the side of the garden bench and slowly struggle to his feet. I followed him into the house.

'Who is it?' he asked.

Cleo shrugged, spooning sugar. 'Markee, you see nobody

89

pass here . . .' she sang to me instead, weaving the lilt of her childhood into mine.

Eldon waved a hand dismissively and picked up the telephone. 'Hello. Yes. Speaking.' I could see him press the receiver hard against his ear. 'Can you repeat that, please.' He shifted the receiver to his other side. Then I saw his whole body shrink until there seemed to be nothing left inside.

Beyond the French windows a robin hopped around the ivy and opened its beak; the spring in its throat uncoiled in a shrill insistent song. I looked back at my grandfather; he was clutching the back of a chair. 'Are you sure it was his plane?' He waited for the crackle in the receiver to cease. Then he put the phone down.

I ran up to him and grabbed his hand. 'Why you crying, Granda?'

I received no answer at the time.

With fire we live, with fire we die. There is no going back. In the crematorium my grandfather's coffin, my mother's and my grandmother's vanished behind a motorised curtain in a succession of heartbreak, suicide and old age; the flames of my father's aircraft, falling, flaring behind each of them, again and again.

The cave – our refuge – slowly filled with the light of a different star. I felt the sun's rays had burnt ulcers in my dream, but my two companions were still asleep. I carried my shoes in one hand and crept over to the entrance. Outside, the dawn was silent. The silence of aftermath: the emptiness of a spent storm. Climbing around to the other side of the rock, I found myself above a great reservoir with a view that dissolved in the morning's marrow mist. The air was moist and chilly. Something in my brain slipped, like a wheel on wet grass. Pictures of my father, and of my grandfather standing against the same landscape, materialised. I imagined the two of them with me, at last finding a place where we might all be close together again, free of discord. 'Look, can you see what I can?'

Eldon always said freedom did not come easy. 'I remember the lyrebird's call to be free of the past,' he would complain. 'But everyone seemed, even in those days, to want to replace one kind of past with another, cabbage with bortsch. I wanted to be an artist of the air not just a Fitzrovian intellectual, you know. An eagle soaring, not a damn peacock strutting.'

From my vantage point I could just make out the jade rim of the jungle on the other side. The flat, calm water was as still as paint, cleansed by the storm that had melded the lake and the sky into one. Clumps of trees, like steep islands, stood in shallow water; the platinum trunks of those struck by lightning bared, with not even an egret to ruffle the slowly evaporating shrouds. The morning light was turning the sky blue. Into my head flew the remnants of an illustration from Eldon's boyhood: grebes, sandpipers, red-shanks, green-shanks, golden plovers, scarlet minivets and high above, a cloud of whistling teal watched by fish eagles, marsh-harriers and brahminy kites. He used to tell me a story of a lakeland ghost who carried a dead child whom she offered to any man she encountered. If the man touched the child he would die, but if he refused to take the child the ghost would turn him into a swine. Eldon said that this was the avenging ghost of the original queen of the island spurned by her cross-water lover for a pedigree mate from the mainland. 'She was our Circe,' he would say drawing a link, like Uva's father, to his other world, 'too often completely misunderstood, demonised for her natural heart.' I wondered if she still lurked there.

Then two gunshots reverberated around the rock.

I dashed back to the enclosure. Kris was outside with a gun in one hand, and a brace of dead bats in the other. 'Yakitori.' He grinned at me and slouched over to a stone slab where he had placed a basin of rainwater. He squatted down and started to skin the bats with his knife, rocking back and forth on his haunches, humming softly to himself.

'They might have heard you.'

Kris carefully peeled back the fur to expose the slimy, stringy flesh of the animal. 'There's nobody here.'

I went inside the cave.

'What happened?' Jaz was hunched up, on the far ledge.

'Kris has been hunting.'

'Hunting what?'

'Breakfast.' I collected the seat-pads and took them out-side. 'So you won't starve,' I added.

Jaz sighed, immensely relieved. 'But, darling, doesn't he know? I'm a vegetarian.'

Further along from where we had slept, Kris discovered a shrine room. Jaz claimed that he could smell oranges, or was it passion fruit? Kris lit a white flowlux that spread everywhere. The rock walls had plaster on them; the passion was sublimated into frescoes.

I had seen photographs of similar paintings in the outdated guidebooks I had studied before coming, but in the cave the images seemed much older than any I had read about. The pale russets, burnt ochres and delicate lilacs hovered in space like early holograms refashioning the contours of the most ancient gods. The figures seemed to shift with every movement of the eye, reviving stories of long-lost times. I imagined old candlelight, flickering; our shadows moving among the protean pigment. These were the memories I had wanted to trace: history, myth, legend all defined in one supple line marrying the seen to the unseen, the spirit to the bone.

'How come this place has not been zapped?' Jaz clung to me. 'I was told all these icons, all the olden-day stuff, got completely destroyed.'

'This cave must not have been known about at the time. Or was forgotten. This whole area was abandoned by everybody.'

Kris intervened. 'We should go now.'

'And where, Kris, are we going?' Jaz detached himself from me. 'Do you even know where to go?'

'Kris will take us to the hills, like he promised. From there I want to get to this place called Samandia. Uva will be waiting there.' I glanced at Kris, but he didn't react. 'We go down south, yes?'

Jaz patted my hand, bemused. 'You shouldn't say that, Marc . . . unless you really mean it?'

'Why? Is it like going down into the underworld?'

Jaz pinched his lips together with his fingers to stop from laughing at another of his Carnival gags.

Near Samandia was the place, Uva said, where the first inhabitants of the island had been awakened by butterflies splashing dew at the dawn of time. The dew formed a lake and their wings a floating stairway spiralling up to heaven. It was here that the first human drowned and ascended to become a god or, according to others, where the first couple – Adam and Eve – were expelled to become real lovers, descending on steps of mortal confetti; their loins swollen, their fingers entwined, their lives ignited. Once a realm of pilgrimage and veneration, it was forsaken after the neutering of the south-west, the devastation of the lower rainforests by rogue missiles and botched nuclear deterrents.

Uva claimed it is purely a matter of chemical balance in the body that makes us feel that the best may be behind us, or even yet to come. Touching my head with her fingertips, she added, 'Or here, if the serotonin is spurting. Right?'

My scalp prickled. 'Yes.'

That was the evening she showed me where the turtles were said to have laid their eggs in the old days.

'Are you sure?' I had assumed it was on the other coast. In the south where the sand was easier to dig and the sea free for thousands of miles.

'There is no other beach,' she said. 'They must have migrated.'

I didn't think so. But then the butterflies migrated. We all did. From one world to another, sometime.

The road plunged through thick, pulpwood scrub. In some places it deteriorated into bomb craters and potholes but the big billowing wheels of the cruiser rolled over them all, flattening brushwood, scattering rocks. Jaz, bouncing in the back, bawled out, 'Why on earth did you ever come to a hole like this, Marc?'

How could I explain to Jaz how much I wanted from this island? How much it represented of a world I had once believed I could never reach. 'My father's father was born here. My father died here. I thought I might find some remains. Something, maybe, about who he was and who I am. I came to learn what my life is all about.'

He leant forward, greedy for more. 'And got enchanted?'

'There seemed no point in going back until I found something, and when I did – how could I?'

'Once you met Uva, huh?'

I looked up at my rear-view mirror and saw Jaz's eyes gleam with vicarious pleasure.

My father's decision to come here, flying east on his own – over the Alps, the deserts of Arabia, the Indian Ocean, over camel humps, golden dhows, catamarans and shoals of singing fish, to a place where sealost sailors believed they would see the springs of heaven rise – began to make sense to me only after I followed him.

Grandma Cleo knew I would do so, long before I did. Whenever I said I wanted to be still, she would rock her head and say it is in my blood to move. 'You'll find child, one day, there'll be a journey you'll have to make. We all have little Argos of our own, dear, you jus' like me.' She too had travelled east, as far, to meet her Eldon in an overcast Britain – an island halfway between their own two warmer ones, hers in the Caribbean Sea and his in the Indian Ocean.

I used to wonder how she and Eldon could have found anything in common: she had come from what she always called the West Indies to support a war of an unknown, and unloving, motherland; whereas he, Eldon, made no secret of his distrust of stories of hope and glory. Once when I came back from a school visit to an exhibition about nations at war, he got quite upset. 'There is nothing to learn from war except the colossal stupidity of men,' he exclaimed. 'Museums these days sanitise the past to make it shine more interestingly – educatively – than it ever should be remembered.'

'But if not for war you wouldn't have met Grandma,' I pointed out, too young to understand the deeper logic of life as it has to be lived.

Eldon had been a well-heeled student when he had first come to England. 'Those days, the poor of the Empire only travelled out of this country, not into it,' he'd explain, drawing for me a picture of a whimsical young man indulging in lazy punts and preposterous motoring jaunts. 'I was the first to get the new super-fast Alvis, you know. Glorious car. Even at the height of austerity I'd happily blow a month's petrol ration on a single afternoon's romp in that magnificent machine.' He'd chuckle at my consternation and flap a hand in the air. 'To get to my age, dear boy, you have to have had some pranks to laugh about.' That was why, he said, he learnt to fly. 'I thought I might one day write a sonnet in the sky.'

In the end though, he admitted, he had never even finished his degree. 'I decided that there was more to life than posturing in a cap and gown. I came to London and learnt to see the history of our times in a different way . . .' He said he had met people who made him rethink everything he had taken for granted before. 'Over warm beer and cigarette smoke they exposed the injustice of the whole colonial enterprise. The Empire they said was an occupying force, a greedy enslaver. Firebrands like Satish and Vernon were ready to punch the lion right on the nose. Independence, revolution, had to be now or never, they claimed. Out of the rubble of Europe they wanted to build the road to our freedom.'

Eldon told me he was never very sure about the metaphors they used, but London did seem then to be a cauldron of cabals. 'Quite a different thing from the collection of villages that the natives imagined,' he added with a slight smirk. 'In those days the Indians here knew even each other's bellybuttons, and the West Indians I met all seemed familiar with every inch of each other's backyards. Even our fellows in town got on well enough for a regular monthly bunfight, you know.'

Then came the war. 'I was called for an interview in some musty office off the Kingsway. "We need you," a big oaf from the Air Ministry announced.' Eldon cleared his throat noisily as if trying to untie a complicated knot inside. 'I told the fellow that this was a squabble that had nothing to do with me. A military brawl between European powers that had been systematically looting the rest of the world. Napoleon, Bismarck, even that woman Victoria had all been, to my mind, pompous bullies craving a bit of their own sun to swagger in.'

His mouth curved down as he recalled the next few months. 'It was only in September 1940, when the bombs began to fall on civilians in London, that I saw that this, like Spain, might turn out to be something really very different.' He met refugees who had managed to escape to England and began to feel a bond with those under siege. Even so, he said, he couldn't bring himself to take life, human life. Influenced by the fringe pacifists of the time, he preferred to give humanitarian help – charity – as foreigners often do in foreign places everywhere. He joined the air medical services, ferrying supplies and wounded patients into hospitals around the country.

It was on one of these missions that he had met Cleo. She had come to England following her brother who had got into the RAF. She had wanted to as well. Eldon said he had been intrigued by Cleo's loyalty for a country that seemed so keen not to reciprocate her affections. I guess an abundance of love was what allowed her to feel protective; showed her how she sometimes might have to sacrifice the more simplistic ideas about what one should or should not do for the sake of something more dear. I can understand that now, but I am not sure Eldon ever did.

Eldon and Cleo were married after the war. By then Cleo had no one else; her brother had been killed in action, her parents were both dead. Eldon was no war hero but, I suppose, she must have seen something in him she recognised. A commitment to her. He sold his fancy Alvis and started a small air service business to earn a modest, but autonomous, livelihood in a country he was beginning to call his own. For a marriage like theirs, he said, post-war Britain despite the soot, the rancid fog and the ration cards seemed to be the only place. By then, he said, he had realised the prejudices of his old home towards a bond like theirs would be even harder to break.

For me my grandfather's inadvertent migration and awkward pacifism was all the more poignant for being rejected by his only son, my father.

When I was a little older I asked Eldon what he believed was really at stake in that early war he'd tried to shun.

'In some ways everything, just as in the conflicts we have today. The dividing line between what is right and what is wrong.' Eldon tapped a column of ash off his cigarette into an empty teacup. 'Look around you now. There are some things people do that are very clearly right, and some very clearly wrong. But there are a great many things we do that are easily confused, especially by ourselves.'

I didn't know what he was getting at. It seemed to me

he was the one confused. I tried to pin him down. 'Do you really think there was an alternative then?'

He brushed aside some specks of ash that had drifted on to the table. 'During those years not everyone understood what was going on, or why. So much was bungled to begin with that the motives became quite mixed up. Sometimes, it seemed to me, fighting was fuelled more by xenophobia . . .'

'That's not really true, is it?' I protested, not quite sure of the word, but certain that it was unfair. Perhaps it was his old age, I thought, muddying the past. 'Anti-fascism, wasn't it? There's no real choice, is there, about tolerating tyrants? You have to fight evil.' Appeasement, I had learned, could not be right. Everyone talked of the need for strength. How you can't give up the fight. I had the beat in my blood.

He looked at me a little in surprise. 'Yes, of course, but the question is how do you do it? By fighting for peace? By violent retaliation? Revenge?' He waited for the words to sink in. Then, in the silence, his gaze dimmed. I felt something retract. He continued in a quieter voice, as if to himself. 'We now know don't we, that if you hit someone to teach him a lesson, the lesson you teach is how to hit.'

I could see that, but I couldn't make sense of it. 'But if you destroy the monster, isn't that the end of it? It's not a lesson.'

Eldon hesitated. 'Have you heard of the Hydra?'

'It was eventually killed, wasn't it?' I replied. 'Not tamed.'

He wasn't listening. 'We have yet to learn the true cost of a bomb: how it accrues over years, decades, lives. I like to believe we can learn – that the young will see more clearly.' He fixed his eyes on me again. 'You must do better in your life.'

I went cold when he said that.

'The art of killing cannot be our finest achievement,' he added, cupping his hands to light another cigarette. 'At least, I could never accept that. Not then, not now. Not even in the most ancient battles of the world. It can't be right. Nothing is inevitable. Not even history. There is always an alternative.'

I remember looking at him then and thinking, he still doesn't know what he should have done; what anyone should have done. The uncertainty had troubled him all his life, and maybe through him also affected my father's. The thought frightened me. I wondered whether all my father's heroic sorties were only a reaction against Eldon's opinions. I tried to imagine what he would have said in my place, what his real convictions were. Why did he not bale out on that last flight? Doubt, it seemed to me then, could be a flaw.

But there were moments of doubt for me too – and culpability, I now know – when clips of muted bombs and missiles were shown on TV. I'd see a child's face, like mine, dodging behind the screen, behind the indiscriminate incendiaries. Eldon would sink back in his chair after watching with me. 'How can they kill ordinary men, women and children for the sake of an idea planted in their heads? Destroy one life to save another? How can anyone believe in such a hierarchy of souls?'

Perhaps, as he claimed, it has something to do with the face you know, and the one you don't. Could it be that easy? Or is there a need to help the innocent, the weak, against the strong? Sometimes maybe we have to work out what is the greater good, however inadequate our mathematics. But he wasn't there to argue with by the time I came to think of that.

★　　★　　★

The jungle expired and we broke out into a stretch of parched fields. The road broadened. We passed a few broken-down houses. Kris peered out and said it was OK to continue. There was no sign of anybody around. We came to a village pond and a schoolhouse. In the centre of the grounds, a tall empty flagpole held up a patch of dirty sky. On the periphery large tamarind trees spread a speckled shade and dry gunge covered the ground.

'There may be something we can use here. Something to eat even,' I said to the others and parked by the gate.

Kris got down and looked around for a food store. I went straight into the school office and opened the cupboard I found in there. It was empty. 'Who would have been here?' I asked Jaz who had followed me in.

'Maybe it is not yet occupied, you know? Maybe it is one of those new villages they are always planning and then forgetting to copulate. I mean populate.' He laughed nervously. 'Sorry. Just a joke.'

I ignored the comment and stared out of the doorway. From the office I could see the whole compound: the rusted earth, the trees, the glimmer of the pond on the other side of the road stuffed with big grey leaves rotting in the heat. Not a single sound stung the air.

Jaz flicked a stray cowlick back and walked hesitantly away. By the window he stopped and seemed to perk up. He shut his eyes and sniffed the air; his crushed bustle rose fetchingly off his haunch. 'This way,' he exclaimed and set off at a brisk trot.

'Where?'

'The perfume, darling, the perfume. Can't you smell it?' He wagged his head in exasperation. Quickening his pace, he disappeared around a corner excitedly invoking young sailors and the scent of sun-warmed smegma.

I was glad to be left alone. I tried to imagine what might have been taught in this desolate school. History? The past choked with wars, disputes, borders as pointless as chalk lines in water. Ideology? Doctrines bloated with blood and bones, perverted by power. My own lessons, I realised, had taken too long to learn; I guess it was nobody's fault but mine.

Then Jaz returned, beaming, with a bedraggled, bare-bodied boy at his side. 'Look what I found.' He had one hand on the nape of the boy's neck and in the other an old-fashioned automatic. He threw the gun to me.

The boy had no shirt, he was wearing torn khaki drills and grubby Shanghai trainers. He had a belt of bullets masking his narrow waist and a brown rag wrapped around his head. His skin was sunburnt. A wispy beard blurred the edge of a pretty, thin face dominated by dark protruding eyes. He reminded me of an early hero of mine whose poster had been on my wall for years: a cover version of his song about shooting the sheriff came to me. Eldon, I remember, did not like it one little bit.

'He says he is a fighter, but that gun of his doesn't even work.'

I tried to open the cartridge chamber. 'What's he doing hiding here?'

'Dreaming of smetana.'

'Where is your camp?' I asked the boy, passing over Jaz's cryptic comment.

'You don't know his language?' Jaz interrupted. 'They don't speak English out here.'

'Why, what does he speak?'

'A junghi-bhasa.'

'And you know it?'

Jaz's eyes lit up. 'I know them all. New recruits sometimes

don't have a city language. They come with all sorts of jungle cocktails. But in my line of business you have to be able to communicate with anyone. The tongue is everything, you know.'

'Ask him, then, where all the village people are.'

Jaz translated. The boy sulked at first, but then grunted out an answer.

'He says they are hiding in the jungle.'

'Why?'

The boy didn't reply when Jaz asked him, but Jaz took the boy's hand in his and gently urged him. The boy listened apprehensively. All at once his whole face seemed to surge with emotion, and words blubbed out. Eventually Jaz turned to me. 'Because of attacks.'

'Who attacks them?'

'He doesn't know.'

'How many of them are there?'

Having opened up, the boy seemed unable to withhold anything from Jaz. According to the boy there were about seventy of them in a settlement. Some were refugees from this village, some from others. Mostly children. They lived in woven huts which they dismantled and shifted from time to time, whenever smokeseed poisoned the air, or wailing. He had no idea how long they had lived in this makeshift manner.

'What's his name?'

'What does that matter?'

'I'd like to know. He must have a name. I'd like to know who he is.'

'But a name will tell you nothing about who he is.' Jaz raised his eyes. He asked the boy, neverthe-less.

'Ismail.' The boy wiped the sweat from around his mouth

with his arm. Ismail meant something to me, although not to Jaz.

'Did he go to this school?' I wanted to know whether he was connected with the place.

Yes, was the answer. Once.

'Is the schoolmaster still here? The headmaster? An imam?'

Ismail looked confused.

'I don't think there are any older men left.' Jaz spoke slowly, as though he was solving a riddle in his young charge's eyes.

Kris fixed the boy's gun, fascinated by its quaint mechanism. He showed the boy how to dismantle the trigger and refit it, how to release the jammed magazine. Only then did Ismail agree to take us to his refugee camp. He sat on the roof of the cruiser, directing the way. As we approached a small hill, gashed by a landslip on one side, a crowd of scruffy children appeared.

When we finally stopped, several of the children came close. They seemed to be peculiarly fearless, but it was perhaps the lack of any reaction, a deadening in the eyes, that gave the impression of fearlessness. One child, a boy with a shaved head, picked up a stick and pretended to shoot us: 'Da-da-da-da-da-da, pschew, pschew, pschew, da-da-da-da-da-da.' The other children observed him, and us, as though they were watchful moths.

Ismail rolled off the cruiser. The younger children scurried up the slopes; the older ones shuffled back a few steps. The boy with the stick pointed it at Ismail and pretended to shoot again. 'Da-da-da-da-da-da.' He then dropped the stick and quickly picked up a handful of pebbles. He moved to one side of the cruiser and crouched. Across the road several empty cans were lined up on a broken culvert. He threw his pebbles hard, knocking one, two, three in quick succession.

Ismail called out and several women emerged out of the bush. They all looked prematurely aged: the nearest, a white-haired mother with a small child tugging at her, immediately began to berate Ismail. She lifted her face, bobbing her chin at the vehicle. Ismail talked back with obvious vehemence, but her expression remained one of suspicion. Only when he reloaded his gun in front of her and she saw that we made no effort to disarm him did she relent. She watched and then she took the gun off him before turning to Jaz. Her voice was sharp but she invited us up into a makeshift community hall hidden behind the trees: a large thatched hut with a few pieces of tatty furniture purloined from the schoolhouse down the road.

The three of us were ushered to a bench behind a table. Ismail half-knelt on a stool. Children and mothers slowly filled the shelter. A red clay pot of water and three cracked plastic cups were placed on the table in front of us. Ismail poured out a small amount of water into each and offered the cups around. He explained to Jaz that this was for us to drink. He looked relieved to be back in a crowd, even a crowd as weary and despondent as this.

Silence seemed to grow between us as we each took our sips. The children watched, awed by the sight of strange men drinking water.

I felt their eyes congregate on me. Even Jaz and Kris were looking for me to say something. What could I say? I didn't want to alarm them, nor did I want us to become unwitting hostages. Eventually I started to tell them about us, asking Jaz to translate; pausing, from time to time, to gauge their reactions while Jaz tried to catch up. They listened without a flicker of emotion as I explained that the three of us were refugees too, escaped from the city on the coast. That we meant no harm and wanted only information: news of danger, soldiers, military reconnaissance, risks.

'Rice,' one of the older mothers interjected from the side.

Jaz brightened. 'She can see we are hungry for rice. Her name is Karuna.'

'Where do they get rice?' I had not noticed any paddy cultivation on our journey.

Karuna explained that the abandoned villages in the area all had granaries which they had emptied into large canisters and buried as secret stores. Last season they had also tried planting red rice – *patchai-p 2462/11*, she recited the name of the variety as though it were a benediction. The numbers were in English. She said they had a small secret mud patch behind the schoolhouse from which they hoped to gather a quick harvest before a passing skyplane picked up the trace and bombed them. Vegetables they grew under removable camouflage thatch with watchers on shift, throughout the day, to let the sunshine in and warn of cloudbursts.

'The children are secret farmers, she says,' Jaz explained excitedly.

Uva's dream children? I wondered. 'Do you think they know her?'

Kris, who was fidgeting on the bench, knotting his fingers around each other, jerked his head up. In his glance I could feel the edge of a knife. He snorted and buried his eyes back in the hard, stamped earth of the hut.

'Uva?' Jaz looked doubtful.

Two of the women left the group and slipped out.

'Ask who taught them how to farm. Where do they get their seed?'

'It's not her. They say they find what they need. They go from one plundered village to another collecting whatever's left.'

Only then did I notice that all the younger women were nursing babies.

Jaz was the one who asked about the men. Karuna told him that there were none. They've been killed or have gone to fight as rebels. They rarely return.

'She says her group is a band of mothers and children.' Jaz's voice dropped lower. 'The bigger kids are stolen by marauders. Six boys and four girls were taken last time. The rest, the weak are butchered, the women who are caught are raped . . .'

The marauders had not been seen for three seasons but the mothers remained vigilant. 'They will be back.' There was no doubt in Karuna's voice. 'They always come back.' The women had no weapons for protection, Jaz was told, but they had learnt to move fast. Ismail had found his gun only the other day and wanted the youngsters to learn to fight. Some of the older ones had already gone to try to find a rebel group to join. The women didn't approve. They wanted Ismail to get rid of his gun. They felt it hampered them, distracted them from better strategies.

As the talk increased, the children began to shift about, looking at each other more than at us, picking at their sores. Suddenly one child started to sing. It was impossible to tell his age: he could have been five, or six, or seven. The voice more hurt than young. Jaz whispered that the boy was singing a nursery song about flowers floating in a pond. A couple of other children joined the chorus, but then the first child came to an unexpected stop.

His mother stifled her sobs in her hands. We learnt that the child had seen his two elder brothers and a baby hacked to death in their home by the village pond. The murderers included a man who had come before. One who had raped her; the baby's father. She still had her life only because she seemed to have died the second time.

The child's eyes were dull, even though his voice had trembled.

Another woman brought forward a slightly older child. This one did not speak any more, Jaz was told. 'Pushpa is ten,' he explained. 'They dread the day she will see her own blood.'

The child's face was beautiful, clear and fresh, but she was lame and her legs were scarred by jagged rips. There were thick welts across her back, clearly visible through the straps of her dress. The marauders had used a bayonet on her, to pitch her from one to another. The woman unbuttoned the back of the dress to show us a pit the size of a fist by the girl's lower spine where her lacerated flesh had been scooped out. It was a miracle that she had survived.

The child twisted her hands together and slipped back behind the woman. I wanted to call her by her name, Pushpa, and promise her a life she need not fear. But I couldn't. She dropped down on her knees and peeped out. I felt ashamed. This was not the world she should have been born to see.

'She has seen too much.' Jaz looked away, unable to stop the tears. 'Her eyes have destroyed her tongue.'

There was no more singing. A warm wind blew through the hut. Karuna offered to show us around the settlement while the food was being prepared. The children filed out, the mutilated remains of an assortment of communities where pain had passed like a malady from one jumbled generation to the next. These were children who had to nurse a numbness to their past; condemned to destroy their progenitors, or remain fractured themselves for ever.

I stayed behind for a few minutes, alone in the hut, unable to shake off the idea that perhaps my own father might have cast the shadow under which these children, or the ones before them, had lived: Lee the veteran bomber. What had he been doing flying over here? Cleo believed one thing, Eldon another. Who was he really helping? I wished then, for the first time, that I hadn't come. This was not at all what I had wanted to learn. With Uva, I had hoped things might become simple; I suppose nothing ever is.

Closing my eyes I can see again the yellow tree on the video behind my father's voice. Why did he not follow his mother Cleo's dancing drumbeat rather than Eldon's suppressed *thakita-tha*? Why didn't I? A different time must mean a different place. And yet by being here now I know this land and its tragic past – its ruined children – become, like the whole of the tainted world, as much mine as anybody else's.

The others had assembled outside a kitchen; the cooks were dishing out a concoction of rice mixed with sour fruit. They had salt-stones, and pastes of chilli and vinegar. Jaz was prattling zappily between mouthfuls about the coloured kafs and bakeries of his underground mall, delighted to have an appreciative audience again, even if only a bevy of grey-haired women with spellbound kids.

★   ★   ★

Later I asked Jaz to help me talk to the oldest woman in the camp – Mukti.

'Questioning, questioning, all the time questioning. Why? What is it you want to know so much?'

'I want to understand what has happened here. Did she ever see fighting in the sky? Aerial bombing? Warplanes shot down?'

Mukti looked to be at least ninety. Her face was puckered into pouches, her skin mottled; she had no teeth, but her voice was strong and her babbling faster than even Jaz's. Her conversation was difficult to follow and left Jaz stranded between the events of the previous century and a past that might have been only days old.

'I don't know what she means,' he complained helplessly. 'Her words are too old. She says that yesterday's water was bitter but better.' The span of her life seemed beyond anything Jaz could imagine.

'Where does she come from?' I asked. 'Where does she belong?'

Jaz understood her to be saying that her father fought in the first war here. Her family, like the whole village, was on one side for that one, and the other side for the next. He asked if she meant the dark war with the cloud. The old woman looked baffled.

'The Great War?' I suggested, but this time Jaz was stumped.

When we were alone, I took Jaz by the arm and steered him towards the edge of the camp. 'You know, I think that place with the school – where at least our Mukti seems to have once belonged – is much older than it seems.' We could glimpse the pond in the distance, and the roof of the schoolhouse. 'That little pond – the tank – could be from the ancient days. The village must have been inhabited and abandoned many, many times.'

'What? Like this? A bunch of people hiding out, scratching a living until they are scratched out. Over and again?'

'This is a jungle that must have been fought over a hundred times, if not more.' I picked up some earth and crumbled the rusty soil between my thumb and two fingers, thinking of Uva's description of warlords thriving on each other's crimes. 'Killing and maiming again and again. It's like some kind of disease.'

'What do you mean?'

'I don't know. I really don't know. Perhaps something in the air? Some infection. Or maybe it's the water so steeped in the past.' I remembered Eldon's poem.

The teardrops of the original inhabitants,
our old gods,
destroyed by invaders,
wreak perpetual revenge on their descendants . . .

The words absorbing, renewing, however dispiriting the story; performing our only true human magic: transforming even pain into a line, a scrap of verse, a rhyme. A greater design.

Jaz plucked at his ear, his larger one, contemplating me. 'You just love that, Marc, don't you? Poems and all that. But the fighting here is not because of some hoary old demon, you know. Don't they fight just as much where you come from? It's just that when people think too much of themselves, their tongues get too fat and they can't talk but shit. That pond may not be anything so mysterious. It's probably just a crater, you know, where some anal dropped another bomb and blew a great big hole in the ground.'

★　　★　　★

In the evening the three of us were given rope beds in a small hut. I asked whose place we had taken, uneasy about us too displacing someone.

'Never mind whose, at least we can sleep in some velvet tonight.' Jaz tested one. He lay down and patted the bed next to his. 'Come, Marc. Take this one. Lie down and tell me a nice, cosy story.'

I shook my head, tight-lipped. I lit the lamp we had been given and adjusted the flame. I didn't have any tales to tell. I had spent too many years holed up alone, stuffing my head with straw and somnambulants, to suddenly start spouting some crappy little yarn for him.

Jaz shifted his gaze and looked out of the open door. The sun had dropped; a few strands of stars showed between the planets unbuttoned in the sky. He seemed to be searching for something. 'How about a big mega-epic then, about a world out of this world, huh, Marc?' His face had an appealing delicacy, despite the multiple layers of souring cream.

'I can't.' I shook my head again. I really couldn't then. I didn't even know where to begin. Not then.

'You are as bad as Kris.' Jaz pouted, more than a little peeved. He opened his pouch and took out a tube of Vaseline. He squeezed a little on to his fingers. 'What is his problem anyway? Does he never relax?'

Kris was outside, scowling at the sky, pacing up and down.

I told Jaz about the first time I had seen Kris. A small cameo to appease him. It was the best I could do. 'Working his sheets of metal, sharpening his tools; making something out of the passing of time: that's what he needs to relax.'

I was about to mention the butterfly knife when Jaz butted

in. 'Like me. My relaxation is also my work, you know. Working the sheets. A bend in the flesh. Shall I show you?' He reached out.

I pushed his hand away. 'Stop it. Do you know where you are?'

He drew back, docile and dutiful. 'Close, Marc, close to the very last planet. The very end . . .'

'What?'

'The end of my tether.' He looked down and solemnly made a mudra with his fingers like a mendicant soliciting solace; then he broke into a laugh, reddening in the glow of the lamp. 'Oh, maybe it is the Amazon then. Is it?'

'Be serious.'

'Why?' His head popped up. 'Why?' Both his eyes welled up. 'If I was, I would cry.'

I realised then that I knew nothing about what he must be feeling stuck in the camp. Perhaps he too was once a waif from a place like this? His face was always expressive of every nuance of every moment, but he never betrayed anything of his past, or the world hidden beneath the eloquence of his body. At that moment he seemed to be clinging to the surface because he was frightened of what lay below. I should have asked him something, but I couldn't bring myself to. I didn't want to get so close.

Outside I heard the hiss of fresh torches being lit, and someone checking the bells and chimes strung around the camp. They were trying, at least, to save what they could of their lives.

I went out to join Kris. A few minutes later Jaz also came out.

'Tomorrow we must go,' I announced to a small group that had gathered around us. Before Jaz could translate there was a scream in the outer darkness. The women sitting at the centre of the camp scrambled to their feet. Several grabbed flaming torches and began to run in circles while others brought out drums from their huts and began to pound them. The rushing flames and the furious drumbeats speeded up frantically until the wailing began to fade, as though a tortured infant was being carried away. Driven away.

'Devil,' Mukti, the old woman, spat out.

At dawn, the whole camp was on the move. Huts were dismantled, carts loaded, cattle harnessed. Jaz learned that the cry of the banshee-bird was believed to be a harbinger of catastrophe. The women said they had to move whenever the devil's voice was heard. Otherwise they'd be attacked.

'Where will they go?'

'They won't tell me. They think the bird is something to do with us. They are terrified of it.' Jaz kept wringing his hands. 'Even Ismail seems to think it has something to do with me.' His lips, his cheeks, his whole face drooped.

I clasped his hands in mine. 'I guess they have lived in terror all their lives. They can't help but suspect us.' I wished I could do something more for them, or for him.

Kris was all ready to go; I led Jaz to our vehicle. We left with no farewell, no words, the wind low in the west.

I drove slowly, unsure of the veracity of old jungle omens. The road disappeared from time to time, but I followed Kris's directions and it reappeared in fits and starts under the wheels. The jungle with its fatherless children faded behind us in twists of temporary oblivion. We travelled through a more arid zone until finally we reached the lush humps of the hill country. The temperature dropped. I stopped the cruiser and suggested we stretch our legs.

'Here?' Jaz shied away from the door like an animal that had been tricked too often.

I said I needed a break and leant back, putting my hands behind my head. The metal tag was still pinned to my ear and I began to fiddle with it. Much to my surprise it came away in my hand; I couldn't stop the smile spreading across my face. 'It's gone.'

'What?' Jaz took a sidelong look.

'It's come off.' I held up the tag like a Lilliputian trophy.

Kris grinned. For a moment he was almost charming. Then he was out of the vehicle, checking the headlamps, the radiator, the aerials.

Jaz leant over and examined the place where the tag had been. 'You'll have such a cute scar, Marc.'

The brief illusion of freedom, unshackled, was bliss. I hadn't realised how much the metal had been affecting me.

Eldon often invoked the hill country when, as a child, I would help him stir the sweetener in his tea on the patio. 'Tcha, just like in the old days, no? A fine cup of tea, roses, trimmed lawns. The comfort of illusions.' Eldon would launch into a treatise on tea production, even though for me, at that age, tea was only something textual – far down the alphabet – rather than a matter of taste. 'Two leaves and a bud, that's what they pick, you see. From bushes about the size of you. Tick, tick, tick.' The old man would pretend to pluck them off my head. 'Then it goes into this huge factory with a wonderful aroma, where the leaves are dried and roasted and rolled and packed off to tickle the fantasies of a global network of humpty-tum addicts.' It took me years to recognise the freshness of that vacuum-packed bouquet he was so fond of, and the reveries it induced, but by then the natural product was on the wane and Eldon's quirky disquisition quite out of date.

I wasn't too happy driving at dusk but Kris was keen that we press on. I switched the headlights on. As we swung around each hairpin bend I saw how the roots of stunted tea bushes gripped the earth. We came to a drive leading down to a factory that, in the fading light, looked as though it had been deserted for decades. Without waiting for Kris to say anything, I turned the cruiser in through the entrance.

'What's this?' Jaz demanded, rested and much more himself.

'A tea factory.'

'Oh, how divine. Happy tea?'

'No. Just tea.' He was incorrigible. I locked the wheel and the cruiser lit the front of the factory in full beam. The windows of the building all had grilles but most had rusted through.

'Just what?'

Kris jumped from the cruiser to check the place out.

I began to tell Jaz how tea had been the major export from the island until synthetics made traditional forms of tea production obsolete everywhere. How tea estates around the globe had turned into tourist museums until real-time museums themselves were superseded by more successful resorts concentrating solely on hedonism . . .

Jaz seemed to be watching my mouth, more than listening. 'Like our underground Carnival?' he asked dreamily.

Jaz knew so little of what had happened in his own environment, to care so little for the past. I wished I could give him the bigger picture in some easy dose. 'You see, then they became a subject of organic archaeology, and the best of them were remoulded into evocation centres. That is until war made the air of some tea-hills too ghastly to breathe . . .' As I was speaking I realised war may not have been the only scourge here; perhaps a reign of autocrats and blunderers coupled to an oligarchy of bloodsucking dorks, as Uva would put it, might have been the bigger curse.

Before I could go on Jaz nudged me. 'Hey, I do like that teapot.' There was a silhouette of a giant teapot at the far end of the factory. 'With a spout like that, it must be happy tea, sweetie.'

At this I lost my temper. I banged the heel of my hand on the steering wheel. 'No, no, no.' I slapped the dashboard. 'This is an ordinary tea factory. Out of commission. Dead. Don't you understand anything? Don't you care about anything?' I shouted at him. 'What the hell am I doing here, I don't know. I am tired out driving this shitty little wagon, trying and trying to give you something of your own miserable history to understand. All to no bloody avail. I just don't want any more sweetie this and darling that from you, sitting there, stroking yourself like God's own head is stuck in your pants. No more, you hear, no more.'

Jaz had recoiled at the outburst. He leaned towards me when I stopped and patted my shoulders gently. 'OK, there, there, simmer down. I was just trying to keep our spirits up, you know. That's all.'

I stared at him, feeling both sorry and upset. It was impossible to stay angry with him. He looked troubled; his flamboyant mask besieged by a thin fuzz of mannish bristles sprouting out of control. I thought again about how the last two days could not have been easy for him. But I was fed up too. I wanted to be alone. I wished I was back in my mousy flat, where I could bask in the comfort of drip-feed dreams and deep screen insulation. It was too late now. I was tired. 'We have to stay here tonight. I'm sorry. I need some quiet. I must sleep.' I didn't care if I sounded like a flatulent old grouch, I wanted to be still.

'Yes, swee . . . tea. Yes, you must.' He spotted Kris skulking around the building with his flashlight. 'Kris will discover a way in. He perked up. 'He'll find us somewhere inside to sleep.'

Kris identified the bunkhouse at the back of the factory and broke into it. I followed him in, brushing aside the cobwebs and gunny flakes. The room was empty. Jaz retreated at once into a corner. He dusted a bit of the floor and sat down with his torch. He started to file his nails using the tiny emery board he always carried with him. Kris offered round a packet of biscuits from the cruiser's emergency rations and then settled into a private meditation of his own, nodding to the rasp from Jaz's fingers. I bit into the digestive and let it slowly disintegrate in my mouth. Our plight had blunted my hunger. Jaz seemed too subdued now. I wanted to comfort him but didn't know how. What would become of him? He was not a cross-country trekker, whatever his origins. And Kris? Always so aloof. What would he do when we reached our destination? Uva, I realised, was the only one who could merge us into any kind of a community.

'This hill road will take us over the central mountains to Samandia, won't it, Kris?' I tried hard to stop my voice from betraying my concern.

Kris, fiddling with his butterfly knife on the other bunk, looked up as though thwarted or something, but then quickly regained his composure. Nothing else gave in his eyes. Watching him open and close the knife I wanted again to hold it; draw closer to her through the metal clone. 'She knows the way there, doesn't she?' I asked, seeking some reassurance. 'Uva?'

From the other side of the room Jaz stifled a yawn. 'Uhuh, sure she knows. She's always been one for the great outdoors.' He put away his nail-file. 'But a rainforest is not really for me, you know. I like a place with a little electricity. A shaving point at least. Some indoor life.' He let out a heavy sigh. 'Your Samandia is not exactly famous for its bars, you know.'

The next morning the sun was a smoky grey. I made my way on to the main factory floor. The place was gutted. All the machines had been removed, but the interior still smelled of tea. It rose out of the floorboards and off the walls and seemed to stain the air with the odour of old ghosts.

In its heyday who would have been here? Sometimes it is so difficult to remember who belongs where, when. Or why. Whose was the labour, and whose the capital? There would have been blasts of hot air and the noise of dryers and rollers; wheels turning, the smell of burning, roasting tea. Narcotic sweat. There was a time when the sound of machines would have filled the air all around the hills. Factories in full swing. A steam train chugging up to the central hill towns. Eldon loved to recall those scenes, complete with sound effects: the clacking of wheels, the hoot of the engine, the constant gabble of conversations between strangers. It was a land full of talk, he would explain. 'Everyone always wanted to *place* everybody else. People would speak to bridge the gulf between them. We had hope, you know, in those days. We all shared the same vision, the same sense of order even if not all our wealth.'

Sanctimonious claptrap, I suppose, but for me that morning there was no sound in the factory, or outside, other than the sound of my own breath misting the air. No words, no birds. Nothing. It seemed as though there was no one else left in the world. Not that I wanted hordes; all I wanted was Uva. A life that was our own.

I tried to picture her journey. Would she have a vehicle? A cart? A bullock? Anything? Survival with no provisions, only a knife for a weapon, I feared would be impossible however close to the earth she might feel. For an instant then I even doubted if she had understood the plan that had seemed so clear to me. But she must have thought as I did: Samandia was our only hope. I remembered the scent of her body as though she had just passed by, leaving a spoor – an urgent pheromonal odour – for me to follow. But is our lake a pool of sorrow now? I see her curled up in a basket of leaves; her head turned in, her neck bared. My arms are empty; they encompass nothing but air, thinning with each passing moment, and yet I can feel the shape of her being from our last embrace: imperfect but strong. The warmth seeping from her leg curled around mine, the curve of her back, and the painlessness of giving in, falling into a new-found deep, dark past. If I could live my life again, I would wish it to be shorter. Let it end with her, quickly, rather than last so long – these interminable hours of her pain; my vigil, remembering, giving breath to our loosening lives.

Jaz appeared. 'Cuppa tea?' He did an extravagant pirouette across the other end of the factory hall.

'You find some?'

Jaz beamed. 'There's this packet.' He held up a small green carton framed by decorative gold leaves. 'It's full of black stuff. Is it original toasted tea, do you think?'

My heart skipped. Eldon's tea.

'Kris will help me make it. I'll bring the tray out to the front.'

A tea tray?

I was just twelve. I wanted to be the first one up in the house. A low snore like the whistle of a turbine emanated from Eldon's room, but by the time I got down the stairs he was already shuffling out. 'Good morning,' he greeted me in a stage-whisper. I followed him to the kitchen which was filled with sunshine. He stood in the light, blinking, then shambled over to the sink and turned on the cold water tap. He let it pour into a plastic washing-up bowl which had streaks of red curry fat stuck to the rim. After the statutory two minutes, he filled the electric kettle and switched it on. He opened a Twinings tea caddy and picked two tea-bags and put them into a white teapot. He didn't bother to warm it. 'I am not a slave to habit,' he mumbled more to himself than to me. 'In any case it is nearly summer,' he observed, as if it made a difference. The beauty of spring and summer for Eldon was being able to spend time in the garden, in the open air, making up for a winter indoors where the central heating dial was permanently fixed at 24 degrees Celsius. His skin would become drier than tissue paper, until the summer allowed it to heal again. Eldon said even the blood flowed around his body a little easier after the honeysuckle bloomed on Mayday. The robin was on the window sill, staring in. 'Hungry, are you?' Eldon lifted a microwave dish cover and picked at the fried belly pork that Cleo had saved from the previous night's dinner. He opened the side window and the robin hopped a couple of steps back, staring defiantly. Eldon placed a charred piece of rind on the window sill. The robin immediately hopped over and picked it up. After another quick stare at Eldon, it flew away, whirring. The kettle bubbled to a roar and clicked itself off, the water subsiding like a passing jet. For some reason I became conscious of his tremendous age then. I felt anxious watching him pour the hot water into the teapot. After a quick stir, he closed the lid. He got two cups and saucers out, making more of a clatter. 'This is my test,' he grinned at me. 'Carrying a tray with two cups, one for me and one for your grandma.' He had invested in extra-large cups so that he could carry them half-full, with plenty of margin for spillage during the bumpy ride upstairs, and yet retain enough liquid for more than a single sip in bed. It meant the tray was substantially heavier. The weight should be helpful, he explained, for finding the centre of gravity, in keeping his hands steady. But that morning his wrists seemed to show the strain. He grumbled about having to do too many infuriating calculations to work out what was best: reduce the volume of tea and thereby the weight; walk faster and reduce the time but increase the risk of a missed step; take one cup at a time. Drink his first, then take Cleo hers, or vice versa. He looked for a moment like a harassed captain of an aircraft, constantly redistributing his payload for optimum lift in a journey from nowhere to nowhere.

I offered to carry it for him.

Eldon snapped back. 'No, no. I can manage. I could fly a jumbo once, you know.'

That afternoon, while I was still at school, he had been rushed to hospital. He had died before the ambulance had crossed the gates. In the coffin his hands were cold and rigid; unshakable. Unfairly steady.

Jaz sipped the brew and screwed up his face in disgust. 'I can see why they've gone out of business.'

In front of us the hills formed a troop of bowed green heads. The once tightly curled tea bushes, slackened with neglect, seemed to be stretching out for freedom. I breathed in the cool air; the fragrance of the infusion, the blend of Uva and my grandfather, was like hope released. I saw Eldon restored with his cup and cigarette; a mist rising, warm and pungent, his eyes lighting up cheered by each bittersweet sip; his hands strong, puffed full of life once more. All the pointless exclamations and vacant phrases that he used to punctuate his days with – his *Ah . . . Bliss . . . I like a cup of strong tea* – slowly began to make a safe and meaningful world again. A lost world of small true affections. One I was just beginning to recover with Uva.

'What's that sound?' Jaz cocked his head, his ear turned towards the suck and chug of a valve pumping air.

The sound grew louder. I looked back at the factory, half-expecting its phantom machinery to be starting up. Then Kris came running from the back, looking up at the sky, circling one arm over his head and pointing with the other at the cruiser. The sound was deafening. I ran to the vehicle and shot it into the parking shelter just before the military Dragonfly whirred overhead, chopping the cool air and swooping down towards the open front of the factory. But the space was too small for its long, vicious rotors and it veered up sharply to one side. It circled the factory once more, and then moved on. The suck-swop died away, although by then my blood was pumping as hard and as loud in my ears.

'Was it them?' Jaz asked. 'Do you think they saw us?'

I didn't reply. The aircraft had no markings; but even if it was not from Maravil, it was clearly a gunship. Kris quickly began to pack the cruiser with our few belongings.

By midday we reached what had been cultivated smallholder land: narrow, old terraces that once might have harboured cabbages, radishes, cauliflowers. Sunshine burst through the bobbled fleece in the sky, creating pools of light and shadow on the road and the slopes; we seemed closer to a thinning above, a hole. But then the cruiser's wheels slowed down. An alarm bleeped from the dashboard signalling a malfunction.

'Is it the gas? Is it the gas?' Jaz rapped his knuckles furiously on the fuel gauge.

I coaxed the cruiser on, working the throttle, the over-drive, even the ignition. The tank was not empty. I thought if we could just get up to the ridge, then we could see where we were, but when we reached it the air was mulled with the dust of collapsed farmsteads and toxic fumes from the valley below. We rolled down the next dip. The road seemed to evaporate before a large arena wreathed in smoke.

'Race-course.' Kris pointed out the white wooden rails of a defunct oval. Two skinny ponies were nibbling at the edges of a smouldering mound of rubbish. Could this be the famous hill town Eldon used to praise for its pure air and perfect turf?

I stopped the cruiser.

'Won't it go any more?' Jaz asked in a voice that seemed more lost than I was.

I said we had better take a look. I couldn't get up any

proper speed. 'There might be soldiers around. We might have to move fast.'

Kris grunted. According to him we were on the edge of a hill town that might still be a Maravil outpost. 'Best avoid it.' He slipped out and opened the engine panel. The steel intestines were too hot to touch. Kris fiddled with a spring mechanism.

'My grandfather understood these things, but I never had the knack,' I confessed, baffled.

One of the ponies reared its head and whinnied. The other one stamped and lunged at it, pushing it out of the way. In a sudden frenzy they went for each other, neighing and biting. A pack of other ponies – black, brown, scorched grey – emerged from behind the festering garbage; they all entered the fray, their hooves pounding the earth. They tore at each other, drawing blood, and charged through the debris, wild-eyed, churning it up and spreading the embers of small fires around them until flames began to flare up briefly everywhere, singeing their shin hair and tails. Jaz stuck his head out of the window. 'What's wrong with them?'

'They want to be rid of each other.' Kris clenched his teeth and set about testing the connectors on a black tube. He then wriggled beneath the vehicle to check the rest of it.

While Kris was underneath, the ponies turned towards us. I could see their ribs sticking out. 'They are heading this way,' Jaz warned from inside. 'You'd better get in quick.' They came up to the side of the cruiser, kicking at each other, rattling their hooves. The grey bumped the vehicle, rocking it. Blood was trickling out of a gash on its face where the flesh had turned inside out. Kris squirmed out on the other side and we piled back in. I tried the ignition. The engine started; I revved it. The ponies in front reared up. Then they broke away from each other and cantered back into the rubbish.

'I don't like those animals. I don't like this place. I don't like it at all.' Jaz locked all the doors.

I calmed him down. 'We'll go now, we'll go.' The cruiser moved sluggishly forward. 'How do we skirt the town?' I asked Kris, easing into second gear.

Kris directed us to a road leading to even steeper hills.

'We'll never make it. We still have no power. Is there no other way?'

'It's the only way. The engine won't fail.'

But with each increase of the incline the cruiser dropped its speed by half, until we were barely crawling up the road. The engine was grinding as if ready to burst; Jaz clamped his hands over his ears and lowered his head. 'Oh God, can't you do something?' I reached for the handbrake but Kris would not let me stop. 'Keep going,' he commanded. When we finally got over the first range, the darkness was impenetrable. The weakened headlights lit up only the verge, the outer tendrils of the giant plants, but not any further, not even the earth of the hillside rising behind those infernal ferns. When the road turned into a hairpin, the lights missed everything and failed at the cliff's edge.

'I can't drive like this,' I said. 'We have to stop. At least for daylight.'

Kris picked up his gun and placed it across his knees. 'OK,' he agreed grudgingly.

I parked the cruiser and turned off the engine.

Kris opened a ventilator flap. 'You two sleep. I'll keep watch.'

Jaz rubbed his eyes with the heels of his hands and settled into his seat. 'I don't think I should ever have spoken to you, Marc. It was a big mistake. I should have given you a bottle of Pin and walked away. Walked right away. Kept you out of my sweet, safe life.' He kicked off his shoes and stretched out under his blanket in the back. 'I had a such good life, you know, in my nice blue bar before you turned up.'

The air was cold in the morning; damp with hill-chilled dew. I had slept collapsed over the steering wheel. Next to me, Kris had also slumped forward and dozed against the dashboard. Outside, moisture seeped out of the grass, making the moss creak. An unbelievable contrast to Maravil with its harsh brackish breeze. I wondered, if I were to utter her name, would the wind carry it to her wherever she lay?

When Kris woke up, he immediately got us moving again. As we climbed higher, the road twisted between trees that became more and more deformed, brutalised by the winds escaping the lower country. Only a variety of moonwort seemed to thrive between the granite rocks. Below the airflow, small pink wild flowers clung to the edge. In places wisps of cloud blew over the road, momentarily obscuring the view of the foothills below, as well as the road winding ahead. We moved slowly, as though every tread on each tyre had to secure a foothold before turning, a groove at a time, up the sharply drawn zig-zag of the road appearing in front of the cruiser.

At the summit, a long stretch of soggy grass reached out for the grey hank piled against the horizon. The cruiser picked up a bit of speed and seemed to roll with the land. The heat, the venom of the lowlands, even the belligerent ponies seemed more than a world away. Jaz was humming behind me, happy again. I could see him in the mirror, supine in the back with his hand trailing out of the window. I wanted to sing too, feeling absurdly hopeful. At last able to believe that the air was unstained, that light was illuminating and that the future was not, in itself, a pollutant.

But then Kris held up his hand. A small waterhole came into view where a big black boulder broke the surface like the back of a beast. There were more rocks on the shore, and two small trees. I slowed down. Under one tree an enormous hawk-eagle hunched, gripping a rodent in its talons. Its wings swelled threateningly as it bent down to tear at its prey with a great hooked beak. I felt my own hunger tighten inside. 'An eagle.' I swallowed hard. 'A real eagle.' I waited for Kris to raise his gun, wanting not its death but that lean, feral meat.

He eyed the bird without moving. 'We are nearly there,' he breathed.

I was surprised. Samandia? It couldn't be.

'Let's go then,' Jaz chivvied from the back. 'Let's go.'

Kris nodded and I, squeezing in my empty stomach, eased the vehicle forward. We rounded another small glen, a rise and a fall, and came to the manicured grounds of a colonial palace. A red and white striped barrier marked the end of the road.

Kris put his finger to his lips. I cut the engine. Silence enveloped us. Before I could stop him, Kris slipped out and padded ahead. He paused by the side of the barrier and listened with his head held slightly at an angle. Then he turned and signalled to us to wait. A moment later he disappeared into the grounds. We watched him steal up the side of the steep garden, weaving in and out of the shrubs.

'Why does he do that? Like a machine he just goes.' Jaz shook his head. 'Why can't he communicate a little?'

I felt anxious but Kris seemed to know what he was doing. I opened my door.

'Wait.' Jaz hobbled into his shoes. 'Now don't you start too. Wait for me.'

I sneaked up to the barrier. The building at the top of the hill seemed to be floating like an empyreal pagoda crested with balconies and glazed ochre tiles. The scene was a picture held in glass. Protected, but with a sense of emptiness that echoed like a loss of heart, a truncated life.

After a while Kris appeared high up on the front steps, his sleeves rolled up, waving. 'He's calling us.' Jaz tugged at my belt.

Halfway up the rough concrete walkway Jaz paused. 'This place *is* really deserted, isn't it?'

At the entrance to the building, two stately black doors dressed with rows of lacquered brass studs and finger plates were open. The walls on either side, decorated with ornamental pillars, were painted a regency red.

Kris, breathing heavily, ushered us in as though into his own home.

'Is there no one here?' Jaz asked, dubiously.

Kris coughed into his hand. 'It's safe.'

Inside there was a courtyard with a garden of ageing rose bushes in the middle and a gallery of delicate fretwork around it; a stone sculpture of a metamorphosing fish occupied the centre. Out of its lips the black streak of a defunct fountain ran.

There were stairs at each corner of the quadrangle and right opposite, a glass wall curtained from the inside.

'What a gorgeous curtain.' Jaz prodded me. 'Aren't you just dying to know what's behind it?'

I looked at Kris. He bowed.

The door was secured only by a simple tubular lock; Kris

had no trouble opening it. Inside we discovered a dining hall with a dozen polished hardwood tables, each with eight chairs whose spindles seemed to imitate the cosmology of an extinct priesthood. Against one wall a sideboard with glasses and a cutlery box; above these a felt-board with notices pinned to it. Jaz went up to the board and read them out aloud as though they were poems on lentil soup, tofu, and mango mousse. He did an excited flamenco stamp. 'My God, can we stay, can we stay?'

Kris nodded. 'Yes, for now we can all stay. There is nobody to stop us.'

The far wall, also of glass, was uncurtained. I crossed the polished parquet floor and stepped down into the lower half of the hall. The view of the land below was extraordinarily pastoral: a vale of blond, gently sloping grassland, dotted with small inky tarns of calm water. The higher ground of the hills on the other side was fringed with tufts of matted jungle. The scene was familiar, even though I had never seen it before. Somehow the pastel colour of the grass, the reflective water, the balance of sky, cloud and soft sweeping hillsides each in its own way seemed connected to a faint glimmering inside my head.

Meanwhile Jaz explored the pantry next door. I heard him open cupboards, larders, eco-fridges and cardboard boxes as if on a shopping spree. 'Look at this stuff.' He hauled out pulse packets and grain bags with huge, bounding exclamations. 'Here.' He passed around a packet of cereal bars. 'Something decent to eat at last.' He crammed a couple, quickly, into his mouth and opened a can of spaghetti hoops.

Kris went to the sink and tested the taps. They worked. He washed his hands thoroughly and rinsed his forearms several times. He shook the water off in slow, wringing motions.

Although Kris seemed remarkably at ease, I was not. I shovelled in some food quickly. 'Why is there no one here?'

Kris shrugged. 'There is no one.'

'How can you be so sure?'

'It was locked up. I had to break in. Trust me. We can stay here.'

I still felt uneasy, but Jaz was delighted. He spooned out more canned slop. 'Here, have some more. This will have to keep us going until I get a proper meal sorted out. Hey, we can have a real party tonight.'

'But somebody must live here. Look at the way it has been kept.' I couldn't understand it.

'This is Farindola,' Kris explained. 'It was once a Chief's retreat but the military have withdrawn. No one will come here now. We can stay. We must stay, until you work out what you want to do next.'

Of course it could not have been Samandia. There were no coconut trees. In the excitement I'd forgotten Samandia was meant to be in the lower country. Much further on. Kris's Farindola must be where Eldon used to go hiking as a boy. What he had called the lunar plains.

'But who has kept it like this?'

'Whoever it was, they are not here any more. No one can come here except on the road we drove along. This is where it ends. I'll rig up an alarm system.'

Kris was right; we needed some time to figure out what to do. I had expected the road to take us all the way, not to come to a dead end. I quickly finished my bowl. 'I'm going to have a look around,' I announced and wandered out. I was glad of his confidence about the safety of the place, even though its immaculate emptiness made me a little uncomfortable.

My first surprise was the room on the floor above.

As I entered I saw, on the wall, a large engraving I recognised from the frontispiece of one of Eldon's books: a portrait of a plump man in a shoulder-first pose with a flag depicting a flattened island unfurled below him. As a boy I had often studied this man's picture while Eldon recounted the adventures in the book. As I examined it once again I heard Eldon's exasperated voice. 'This fellow from England spent twenty years on our island and wrote a whole bloody book about it; I've spent sixty years on his and haven't even written a damn letter.' His old friend Anton who was with him sniffed ungraciously. 'That's that book that inspired Robinson Crusoe, no? Our fellows didn't know what they started when they held that bugger prisoner.'

I went over to the glass case in the centre of the room. It was filled with fishing reels and gaudy, feathered flies. In one corner there was a pocket-sized pamphlet: *Trout Fishing on Top of the World*. It had a photograph on the cover of a family gathered by the banks of a stream. I imagined Eldon as one of the party; the youngest boy: scowling at a fishing rod, already concocting some wild exploit to relate in his later years.

The light outside changed. A soft hill rain misted the windows forming small elongated drops. Lower down the glass they converged into a more crowded map of minute coalescing lakes distorting the view of the black tarns below – the trout ponds, I reckoned. The rain drifted down the hillsides. The sealed room was quiet but, watching the mist and the moisture, I felt that even in the open there would be no sound to this rain.

★   ★   ★

In our new abode, Kris seemed to come into his own. He identified the keys to every lock, and allocated each of us a bedroom as though he was the proprietor of a country inn.

Mine was on the corner of the second floor. After being reacquainted with the old engraving and having imagined Eldon outside as a boy, I felt more at ease. I was content to walk alone. As Uva would put it, our independence and our interdependence were locked into one embrace. An embrace, I now long for.

Cold, thin cloud entered the open airy corridors of the building in drifts, blowing a welcome dampness that clung to every surface even my clothes, my skin, my hair. Down in the inner rose garden a small bird was pecking furtively about the statue in the centre. It had a striking cerulean breast, and a head crested with busy yellow streaks. For some reason I was glad not to be able to identify it. I listened hard, leaning over the parapet, hoping to catch the notes of its song, but there was only windrush, the hush of mist turning into moisture, a beak rapping. Then a trickle of water came out of the mouth of the statue. It had to be Kris at work, I reckoned, turning yet another system on: it was as though he wanted to settle in Farindola for ever.

On the landing, at the top of the stairs, I found the door bearing the number he had given me. It opened to a large room with a bed, a desk and chair, a bookshelf and a wardrobe. Another door within led to the bathroom. I turned and was startled; it took me a while to recognise the dishevelled figure in the mirror. My face had got quite brown and was caked with dust; my hair was matted. I needed a wash. Kris had said that everything was solar-powered, even the hot water. I turned on the tap over the bathtub. The chrome pipes, peppered with age, spluttered and hissed at first but within seconds settled to a fast-flowing stream of warm, slightly yellow water. Even the sound of it was a comfort: the gurgle of water on water amplified by a cast-iron drum. The whole room turned humid as the bath filled. I tested the temperature with my fingers and added a bit of cold. Then, stripping off each grimy garment in logical succession, I sat on the luxurious commode until steam entered every pore. Afterwards I lay full length in the hot frothy water with only my face and my knees protruding. I turned the taps off with my toes and let my feet sink to the bottom. A thin skim of thoughts swirled like rainbow-spills on a wet road. A warm current wafted up the insides of my legs, as she might slide to sheathe me.

I rubbed coconut oil down her arms and legs: a muscle leapt beneath my fingers. Her skin was sometimes as tight as a drum, as if she was all bunched up and ready to fly, and at other times it seemed as capacious as the surface of an ocean.

In that bath, that evening in Farindola, the memory of her seemed somehow to revolve within every other thought that came to me, and yet I was unable to hold on to her. Each time I tried, the sense of her, the essence of her, seemed to slip away; disappear, just as each time my fingers moved towards a patch of coloured bubbly water, it floated further out of reach. The time we had had together was like a dream, eroding, conforming as all our memories do to the shape of our immediate needs. Up in Farindola, although something of her straddled my innermost nerve, I simply could not clasp her, cherish her, as I wanted to. When I closed my eyes I saw Jaz instead, submerged in his own bath, with a wet flannel on his face and his swollen shiny glans breaking the spumy water.

★   ★   ★

When I came out, later, the sun streaked briefly again across the western sky. I heard Jaz chatting to Kris in the rose garden and went down to join them.

He was immaculate in a crisp maroon sarong and a narrow indigo tunic. His hair was gelled back, his freshly depilated chin and cheeks glowed in the sunset. His eyes were larger than ever; the lids freshly painted with azurlite and a frit of silver.

'Nice costume,' I smiled, conscious that the clothes I had put on after my bath had yet to be cleaned, but wanting his pleasure at least to last.

Jaz pranced around delightedly. 'You like it? I found these fabulous clothes in my room. Feel the sarong. The threads are so exquisite. I love it. And the tunic is divine. It fits perfectly, like it was tailor-made for me. And there was a gorgeous kit of make-up. Did you try the jojoba shaving stick?'

I chuckled and teased him about how someone must have known he was coming.

'What? You think they know?' He ducked down and spread out his hands, his fingers wide apart and curving up at the tips. 'You think they might be watching us?'

'I was just joking. Don't worry.'

'But they might be out there. My God, maybe it's a trap.'

'I don't think so,' Kris mumbled behind him.

'But you don't know.' Jaz kept his shoulders pulled in, compressed. 'I like this place, you know. I really like it here. I don't want any bang-bangs.'

The sun disappeared. Swiftly, in the afterglow, shadows seemed to grow. Jaz grabbed my hand. 'Why is it so dark?' He called out to Kris. 'Can't you do something? What's happened to the lights? I thought you'd fixed them?' But even as he spoke the flowlux began to glow along the corridors. They were slow to brighten, but the faint rims of light were enough to pacify Jaz. Even the rose beds had lights peeping through. Kris led us up the stairs. From the balcony we could see the walkway light up, and another string of pearly lights marking out the edge of the garden. Jaz clapped his hands happily. 'A magician, darling. I told you. A real magician, this man. Look at it: a lovely beacon, don't you think, for dear Uva?'

Kris stiffened, his face set hard as it did whenever Uva was mentioned.

'You don't think it will attract the wrong people, do you?' Jaz added, after a slight hesitation.

'We won't be disturbed,' Kris assured him gruffly and turned away.

Jaz took my arm, relieved. 'In that case, I think it's time for me to make us our first dinner. You boys can open the gin. There's a *huge* bottle in the lounge.'

I prised myself away. I wasn't ready. 'You go ahead. I'll be along in a while.' Although Kris seemed to have allayed Jaz's fears, in the dark I felt my own disquiet, for no apparent reason, return.

I decided to explore the inner lip of the garden; to follow the walkway around the building before going to the dining room. Along the way I noted evidence of a devout gardener: freshly painted trellises, young cuttings recently planted, protected old trees.

Farindola seemed to have been created with real concern: the natural viewpoints, the curvature of the land, all enhanced rather than diminished, and everywhere a desire to accept the past expressed in terms of circles and spirals, care and conservation.

Beyond the gingko tree lower down, I reached a clump of rhododendrons: sprays of purple buds lifted upwards as if in perpetual offering to the gods of the mountains. One of Kris's lamps, threaded through the bushes, blinked in distress. A loose connection, I guessed. This, I told myself, might be something I for once could fix. A nice turn of practical success – a bit of handiwork – to relate to the others. I located the cable and followed it into the thicket. The bushes, disturbed, gave off a rich, nauseous smell: night breath, our life blood, earth's own profanity exhumed. I tugged the cable and the branches juddered. I pulled aside a clutch of leaves to free it. I thought I knew what to do; how to use my instincts, shake, fiddle, fix. Strip a lead, splice a tape, that had been my forte. I broke a stem to make an opening I could crawl through, and got down on my hands and knees. Then, in the flickering light, I saw a claw. At first I assumed a clump of twisted twigs had tricked me, but then I realised it was a hand. For several seconds I couldn't even breathe. The bony hand with its gnarled fingers, its dry crinkled skin, looked petrified. Tentatively I moved another clump of leaves and exposed the rest of the body: that of a hunched woman with a knot of hair steeped in blood. The blood had just about congealed along the slit cut into her neck. My hand must have shifted the cable into position; the bulb next to me buzzed, as if about to short, but stayed on. I could see black globules stuck to the pasty flesh. The seam of her cardigan was thick with coagulated bits snagged by the coarse brown stitches. The earth reeked as I knelt before her. I tried to haul the body out but I couldn't shift her limbs to get a proper grip even though the rest of her body had not yet completely stiffened. The arms were cold; iced inside.

Her head was at an odd angle. Something snapped, muffled by the dead flesh. My stomach turned. Sick surged up the back of my mouth. I had to pull up my shirt over my mouth and nose to stop from vomiting. It was worse than seeing the red puddle swell on Kris's workshop floor. This corpse was in my arms. I forced myself to look at her face. Her ruined mouth gaped open revealing a few misshapen, badly stained teeth; her eyes were squeezed dry by her collapsed wrinkles. My grandmother Cleo was probably older when she died, but in death she had lost all the markings of a close-held life. In her coffin she had become younger than I had ever known her, her skin stretched and smoothened beyond recognition by the undertakers. But here death had robbed this old woman of something more in its violence. I looked up: the whole place was much darker than before. Further along the walkway several of the lamps had gone out.

It wasn't long before I detected the second body, that of a parched elderly man who must have been her husband shoved into a bed of orange azaleas. His fate had been as brutal and as disconcertingly recent.

When I stepped inside the dining room, my hands were shaking.

'Are you cold?' Jaz offered me a glass of gin. 'Here, have a drink, while I finish up. The kitchen is my domain, OK?'

I grabbed the glass gratefully, and took a quick swig. Jaz bustled about, whistling and warbling as he set dishes on the table, arranged flowers, lit oil wicks. I drained the rest of the drink and went to wash my hands.

I went over everything that had happened since we had arrived: how Kris had darted ahead up through the grounds, his assurances, the pristine state of the building, the lack of any sign of danger. It was clear to me that Kris must have murdered the old couple, but I couldn't bring myself to say anything to Jaz just yet. Not only because the killing would upset him, but because it would defile for ever the evening Jaz had been so looking forward to. I wanted to protect the moment, even though I could do nothing for the dead. There was no need for their deaths, surely? The old woman and the even older man could not have been much of a threat.

I dried my hands on a towel which I then chucked to one side. I poured myself another drink – half a tumbler of gin – and went out on to the balcony. The sky was scored with falling stars. I wondered where Kris was. Whether perhaps I should tell Jaz now, after all, before it was too late. But what had been done could not be undone. What good could it serve?

Jaz called out, 'Come and sit down. Sit, sit.' He steered me to a table set with maroon place mats, elegant decorated china and stainless steel cutlery. Kris appeared with three sparkling goblets in his hands. 'Perfect. Perfect. You found even wine,' Jaz cooed. 'Then we are ready,' he proudly announced. His face was shining and he looked almost as ebullient as he had been in the Juice Bar when I had first set eyes on him. 'We could live here for ever,' Jaz crooned. 'There's loads of stuff. Everything you can imagine.'

I forced a smile.

Kris used a mechanical corkscrew to open the wine. I watched his fingers – stained with engine oil – close around the neck of the bottle. The grapey air of a previous decade escaped without a sound as the cork was released; I felt a tremor of revulsion as Kris filled each goblet with blood. Nodding politely he passed one to Jaz, and another to me.

'So, who do you think stayed here?' Jaz asked me, warming to the occasion. 'You find any clues?'

I tried to suppress the image of the murdered woman's face. I looked at Kris, but could not catch his eye.

'Kris says whoever was here has gone for ever, but I don't understand how. There's fresh food, you know. I found garlic. And even some really sweet, tiny strawberries in a dinky little punnet.' He giggled.

I said nothing. I picked up the goblet and, with a grimace, drained it. The wine was musty and smelled like farmyard shit, but I wanted it.

'Hey, not so fast, mister. You need some food inside you.' Jaz quickly served out his dish of semolina and chick-peas. 'Here, you really must have this, Marc, before you guzzle any more of that stuff.'

I ate furiously, incensed by the clatter of cutlery around me. I poured myself more wine. The food was going fast. Only after downing a third glass did I slow down enough to speak. 'I think Kris is right. This must have been a retreat once, before the base shifted. There would have been just an old caretaker couple left here to look after it . . .' I paused, but there was no reaction from Kris. 'Originally it must have been a place of peace. Tranquillity.' I pressed on, determined to force a reaction. A confession, I suppose. 'This must be the only place where real regeneration is still possible.' I wanted to be effusive. If she were with us, I told Jaz, Uva would be thrilled to find this historic architecture, the self-sustaining technology, the balanced gardens and the wilderness so dutifully nurtured even if only for the benefit of a few. I got carried away, briefly, imagining her walking outside.

'So where are they, then, these lucky folk? Do you think they'll ever come back?'

I was nonplussed. It was difficult to focus on what I should say next. 'Depends on what really happened here.' I tried again to draw Kris's attention.

Jaz laughed out loud. 'Not that past business again, Marc? Please.'

'There's no tomorrow without yesterday,' I said quietly. Everything was turning murky. 'The future is inside us. The tree is in the acorn.'

'Oh yes, I know all about that.' Jaz shuddered with a deep throaty laugh. 'And the acorn in the big-big tree, but what has that got to do with this place?'

Kris finished his food and began to clear up. 'He knows how everything works here,' Jaz explained admiringly as Kris disappeared with the plates. 'He's even fixed the old dishwasher in the kitchen.'

'Good. I'll go give him a hand. You just take it easy here.' I decided to confront Kris alone. I tried to smile at Jaz. 'It was a wonderful meal.'

'Kris is the one who found the place.' Jaz snuggled down in his chair. 'He really is a darling little fixer, you know.'

I took my wine with me into the kitchen. When Kris looked up I raised my glass, unsteady but resolute. 'Cheers.'

He made a slight sign of acknowledgment while cleaning his plate into the bin. The others were already stacked, methodically, in the dishwasher.

'We are stuck here for a bit, I guess. It'll take a few days, huh, to strip that engine right down? Do you think you'll be able to fix it?'

He pressed the door of the old appliance and checked that it was shut properly. 'Gas might be a problem.'

'Anyway, this is a great place you brought us to.' I couldn't stop my face from sliding into a sneer. 'At least we can get some rest, have some comfort until we work things out.'

He clicked the knob on the front panel to select a programme.

'You think Jaz is right to worry?' I was trying hard to control myself. 'You think anyone will come back here?'

Kris's head moved slightly to one side as if to catch the sound of a hidden lever.

'What about the caretakers?'

Only then did he finally look up. But still he said nothing.

My chest was puffed-up. I was hot and thirsty. I swilled back the rest of my wine. There was another open bottle on the worktop; I sloshed more into my glass and drank it faster than I had intended, trying to swallow the words I knew even then shouldn't be spoken. But I couldn't stop them from bubbling up, like froth out of my mouth. A drum was beating in me.

'I saw them, Kris, I saw them. A tiny old woman and an old, old man. I saw their throats. Why? They'd have just done whatever we wanted, wouldn't they?' The complicity I felt made me bluster. 'Why did you have to do that, man, why?'

Kris turned to pick up the last of the dirty dishes, ignoring me.

I shouted at him. 'Hey, wait. Don't turn away. I'm talking to you, man. Listen.' My voice was louder than it should ever need to be. The alcohol had plugged my ears.

He hesitated. He looked back at me. There was a shadow over his face, but even so I could see him tense up.

'You know Uva. You know all about her, don't you?' I demanded. My mouth hurt, my breath hurt, I stared so hard that my eyes hurt. I don't know why I brought her into it, but I couldn't help it. I was sure there was a link between them. 'Do you love her?' The words spluttered out of my mouth. I knew I was asking questions that Kris would never answer, but my head was spinning. I lunged forward to grab him by the shoulders. 'Tell me. Or did you murder her too . . . Tell me, you . . .'

With one swift move, Kris deflected my hands and knocked my glass to the floor. It burst, splashing the wine between us. Kris's lips disappeared into a sharp straight line and a stream of mercury seemed to flow into his hands. His butterfly knife was unfolded.

From the other room, Jaz called out, 'What happened? What broke?'

We stared at each other, stupidly face to face. His cheeks tightened; he opened his mouth a crack. I could smell the wine on his breath as he forced each word out, crushing every syllable into the next. 'Yes, I know her, but it has nothing to do with you.'

I wanted to shove the words back in his face and push out my own but, in the end, I had to look away. I thought he would kill me too if I even opened my mouth.

The next morning I emerged from my room charily, my mind still in turmoil. It wasn't just the corpses or the drink; I had lost control. I worried not only for myself but for Jaz, for everything. I couldn't tell what was right and what was wrong. I didn't know what to do about the bodies. About Kris. Was he a danger to us all? I made my way, gingerly, to the dining room where Jaz was eating. When he saw me, he brandished a piece of toast. 'Want some?'

'Where is he then?' I asked.

'Kris? By the time I got up he had already finished digging

up a new flower bed, or something, in the garden. He had a big spade with him. He's gone out into the jungle now. Maybe he wants to cultivate that too.' Jaz stuffed a buttery soldier in his mouth and then examined his nails minutely. 'I really must do something serious about these today,' he declared between chomps.

I swallowed two large glasses of water. It was all I could manage. Burying the bodies was not enough. Something more had to be done. I went and picked up the gun from beside the cutlery tray.

'You planning on hunting some beasties, like our Kris?'

I steadied myself against the table. I clipped a spare magazine of bullets to my belt, not quite clear what to do, but resolved to do something. 'I'll see you later.'

'You should eat while you can, you know.' Jaz reached for my arm, but I brushed his hand aside. He was not my sage.

From the docking bay at the back there was a footpath that led to an old iron turnstile. It clicked as I let myself in. The path continued down to the flat land through which a small stream ran. Small pinched yellow gorse flowers grew beside it. I looked for some sign of Kris, but there was nothing to suggest which way he might have gone.

Mist seeped out of the jungle wrapped around the higher slopes. Within moments the sunshine disappeared. Clouds scudded along the ground until the whole place resembled a primitive battlefield; the trees lower down the hillsides were tilted like wounded heroes. I had an urge to use the gun. As a child I always wanted to be a warrior who could avoid my grandfather's censure by running low, crouching close to the ground in an imaginary world of clean theatrical wars spurred by cute computer games, heroic films, and the mysteries of my father's foreign adventures. On my little walks with Eldon, it was easier to imagine the enemy behind the roses, or hidden in the evergreens, than in the slipstream of the aircraft up in the sky where my father flew. Napalm tossers and suicide bombers, like kamikaze pilots, belonged somewhere else entirely. We were in the realm of cream teas and maids of honour. Fantasies of safety.

At the stream I splashed a handful of icy water on my face. Every drop was crystal clear; I could see new moss on the pebbles at the bottom.

Eldon had always argued that no one could really justify the taking of another person's life. But kneeling there I wondered, perhaps the dead couple were not caretakers. Perhaps they were retired despots. Experts in their day with truncheons, electrodes and flames. Torturers and murderers. Terrorists. Their victims, then, would have been avenged. Perhaps that is as it should be. Or maybe Kris knew of dangers that I did not. He had already killed two soldiers in our defence. Was that also wrong?

A sinewy brown swerve between the rocks in the water twisted into the flash of a wild trout. Wouldn't it too value its own life more than those around it?

I had a difficult calculation to make. I got to my feet and followed the path around the side of a small hill, and then down to the first of the tarns. A placid pool that seemed to absorb effortlessly the turbulence of the stream gushing in through the stone sluice. I wished I could too.

From the other side of the pool the stream flowed on more sedately, stretching long strands of brown weeds into the second tarn lower down. I walked beside it, the memory of the night salting each crevice inside me, hardening me for things that I didn't know were yet to come. I wanted to purify myself in the warm sun wishing that light in itself was forgiving.

The morning sun returned, ripened. The mist and cloud vanished. The air thickened, slowed down, softened into something summery. All around the ground uncovered itself. My thoughts slowed down; the sky widened. Eldon appeared, a young boy hiking about the vale. Was this what my father came looking for: the fount of Eldon's youth? The dreamland of all those childhood stories that the old man had nourished one generation after another with? But the colours and shapes, the climate and temperature, seemed much more mine than his. It was as though I had arrived somewhere I had been before, rather than he. Perhaps that is what we all discover. That we've been here before. That everything we do has been done before.

I stopped moving and there was complete silence. The air itself seemed to doze, waiting. The stream rested motionless on the surface. Nothing moved. Not even a blade of grass. Then, a few steps further on, I noticed the sound of water dripping through the hillside, moss oozing. The green, the growing, came from giving, not taking. What did Eldon really give me? What did Uva give me? Wasn't it the idea that things could be made better? That nothing was impossible, that our lives should not be limited.

The path forked. I took the left, hoping that Kris might have taken the other. I realised that the vague idea I had had in going after Kris was wrong. He had his karma, I had mine. It was not for me to judge him.

I passed the next tarn and the one after that, observing the occasional popple and threading, in my mind's eye, those iridescent fishhooks in the glass case indoors. One life ends, another goes on. I saw then that even if Kris had shared a life with Uva, it did not matter. It did not have to alter what we had found together. Or so I thought I must believe.

A frog croaked. A moment later my eyes lit upon a single

white moth. Nearby, on a piece of granite, a solitary fly rubbed its diamond wings; grass seed swayed. The sounds of wildlife rekindled Uva's vision: flowers springing open, feathers unfurling. All God's creatures dancing, spinning the earth and binding us together in one eternal space. Yes, all of us.

I followed the trail into a forest of eucalyptus and pine. The narrow red clay path rose up through a screen of rubbery vines and twisted, spongy trees into a final patch of grassland before reaching the end of the plateau. The last stretch was a hundred metres of frenzied vegetation; wave upon wave of trees and bushes piled into each other as though a spate of growth had been arrested in mid-flight: brought up short at the end of the world. I reached a rock ledge with a wall of cloud right up against it. Thick vapour hurtled from below. Surging up to the height of the tallest trees, it then curled in and dissipated. The jet of white was tantalising. I wanted to step out into it and be lifted off the edge of the earth. To leave all my tangled emotions behind and give myself up to the wind. But I didn't. I stepped back and watched the trees drip with precipitation.

Then, unexpectedly, the cloud cleared; in the brief moment before the next one shot up, I caught a glimpse of the lowlands two thousand metres or more below. A carpet of green. Samandia.

There had to be some way I – we – could get down to the plains, the forests, the aboriginal lake. It was closer than I had expected, as a bird might fly. Fresh clouds thickened quickly, obscuring the scene once more.

After a while I followed the cliff path around the outcrop of trees to where I thought the cloud might be thinner. It brought me to a clearing: a concrete arena with two large domed sheds on the far side and a tube of iron – twin rails

– that ran up to the edge of the precipice. I made my way cautiously along the perimeter, avoiding the painted markings on the ground.

The first hangar was empty, but in the second one I found an aircraft. A flying machine made in the shape of a giant peacock.

IV

FLIGHT

T HE STORY of the giant peacock – the sky chariot from
the island's most mischievous myth – was immortalised,
for me, in the video I had found in my flat last winter: my
father's only real bequest.

In the opening shot, fresh yellow leaves fill the screen.
Birds trill between them in a pulsing tapestry of song more
real to me than the rattle and squeak of the tape itself as
it plays, again and again, in the small grey study that was
turning into something between a shrine and a crucible
day by day. The camera pans the bloodshot clouds, and
my father begins a true traveller's tale, his bottled voice
promising a brilliant world of renewed life. 'This is what
I see every morning from my balcony.' He zooms in
on a tree full of bright yellow flowers, a vast cage of
golden chains. 'This is the most wonderful tree in the
neighbourhood. Dozens of different birds come to it. And
if you look carefully you'll see them, climbing and turning,
singing and hiding everywhere in the blossom. Marc, you
would love it.' He then turns the camera on himself. 'This
may be right in the middle of town, but it is magical . . .'
His face beams, never to grow old. Each time I see it I
pause the film, unsettled by the knowledge that too soon

my own age would surpass his and head inexorably towards my grandfather's.

'This evening I'm going to the grand exhibition that has opened for the Independence celebrations.' My father grins. 'I'll film it for you.' One of his teeth is chipped, breaking the line in his mouth a little. The TV screen then fills with a crowd of people: figures in sarongs, trousers, dresses slowly moving in a wrinkled line. The picture is grainy, reddish, the light low, but festive illuminations garland the trees. His wry comments seem to be jokes directed especially to me, his only child: 'Everything here is now topsy-turvy. You see, to get in we have to go in around the back. The entrance is the exit.'

From the very first viewing my heart is virtually in the camera as it moves shooting from elbow level, as though my father is cradling it, like a hunter, as he walks. The camera is jostled and the picture jumps from side to side. I want to reach for his invisible hand, to steady it with mine. Older, perhaps even wiser now. But whenever the camera zooms I feel myself zoom too, a child again, next to my father, watching some chef chopping roti, or a craftsman twirling a lathe. 'This is a huge exhibition, food of all kinds, stalls, shops and, of course, all the Forces. Over there behind the police band, is the army.' Then the film cuts to a fuzzy blizzard where I yearn to take my place, like my father, everpresent between a tapehead and a cathode ray. Something more than imagining, but less than memory. An electronic chimera like any of the swarm of other youngsters there with him in the next frame, squashed into a stockade packed with weapons and army vehicles. 'Pay is good in the army.' He lowers his voice. 'But the military needs to aim at the younger generation: for kids it's the cool commando uniforms, the fancy knives, the sheer power of the tanks and the big artillery guns that are more attractive. Marc will understand.' He homes in on a hut with camouflage nets draped over it. 'That's the war box,' he explains. 'Inside they have simulated a combat scene. A virtual reality show. Mortars blasting, machine guns, tanks crunching through the forest. The kids love it.' A queue of children, some as young as I had been when my father made the video, stretches right round the small compound, wriggling to get in. 'They are trying hard to make this business exciting. The idea is to turn it into a sort of Disneyland for them.'

Then the camera cuts to a long thin glider mounted on a grey platform. A small group of boys are listening to a pilot demonstrating the controls inside the cockpit.

'This shot is really for Dad, if he ever comes around to watching it.' His voice falters. 'He took me up in one of these – a K13. I'll never forget that first flight. It was the first time he let me pilot. I really felt he had some faith in me then. That was when I learned that with confidence – if you knew which way the wind blew – you could control everything. You have to, otherwise you fall out of the sky, isn't that so?' He looks appealingly at the camera as though he expects to find Eldon there. I understand what he wants, even if Eldon never did. But I could not imagine myself up in the sky with him; with either of them.

For me it is the scene with the great wooden peacock with its rich mix of history, legend and myth that is the real moment of communion. Even the quiet entrance to the air force arena, a square of restrained flowers and orderly hedges, is potent with promise. When the huge bird with its outstretched wings, each feather carved like a petal, fills the screen I, like my father, am awestruck. 'The first aerial chariot', my father rolls each word with wonder, carrying me, his son, with him into a fabulous past of magic heroism and fantastic celestial odysseys.

As the lens widens to show the pretty coloured lights strewn along the hedges like landing markers, two young men drift into the picture, their brief conversation captured for ever by the camera.

'This is the first aircraft. Not bad, no?'

'But I thought those Wright brothers were the buggers who made the first plane.'

'No man, that was much later. In America or somewhere, no? That was just a nineteenth-century thing, no? Our fellows did this a long time before that.'

My father's quiet laugh bubbles out of the tape then, spilling a moment of paternal delight into my wanting, waiting life. 'Separating myth from history is impossible now. Everyone has a fantasy with which to stake their claim for the territories in our heads.' He pauses. 'Who can tell where the truth lies?' The picture goes dark for a second and I wonder, every time, what he was really up to in those last months. Was Cleo right about his mission of mercy? Or Eldon, who saw only delinquency? Then a plaque comes into focus. 'Look at this board: it even gives a date. It claims two islanders were the brothers who invented this Trojan peacock, in 2525 BC. And that it was used to bring the most beautiful woman in the world to this verdant paradise, away from the tedium of a husband whose only passion was playing with bows and golden arrows.' His disembodied voice takes on a sudden urgency. 'A voyage of *love*, like all our journeys. Next week I'll have some time to go to our place on the coast. Remember the wildfowl centre? On the next video I send you'll see what it looks like now.'

But there was no other video. Those words to my mother

were his last to any of us. Every time I heard the passion glow in them I felt my blood ignite.

'I've found something,' I called out to Jaz in the courtyard. 'Come with me.'

Jaz's face lit up. 'Kris, here he is.'

Kris, who was busily cleaning a steel apparatus, ignored us both.

'Look,' I started but then wavered, catching sight of his knife. Ever since I had met Uva I had come to believe that all our actions were somehow always measured against an idea of what they ought to be. That there was a purpose and a pattern, that our lives were ethereal links in a great sacred chain that must not be broken. But in Farindola I began to see I might have been misled. That there is only chaos before us whichever way we look and that we must each find our own means of survival in a world of mounting disorder. Eldon must have known it. And Cleo. Why do the old hide the truth from the young?

Kris squeezed some oil into the hub.

I took a deep breath. 'I'm sorry about last night. I guess you must have done what you thought was best. I know that now. Let's put it behind us, forget it. I'm glad that you've buried them. Now come and see what I've found.' It was feeble, I know, but it was all I could do.

Kris continued to clean the metal without a word.

'It's quite an extraordinary machine.' I made a last effort to entice him.

'Machine!' Jaz made a face, pressing the tip of his nose flat with his thumb.

Kris put away his contraption and stood up; his mouth still clamped tight.

Only when I showed them the hangar and Kris saw the aircraft, did he finally give in. His whole face softened. He stroked the graceful curved neck, the fuselage trimmed with thin strips of varnished coconut wood, flecked with bits of beaten copper and riveted with brass studs; he practically swooned. While Jaz flounced about the tail, Kris took his shoes off and climbed up the moulded footholds to where the hollow wing was fastened. He tested the white mastic which, like cartilage, lined the join; he seemed pleased with its texture and went on to check the seals around the door at the nape of the bird. The aircraft had been designed to carry two people: a pilot and one passenger in a feathered cockpit carved out of the peacock head. Most of the body was moulded out of titanium or fibreglass, but made to look like real wood, and copper, at its most sensuous points: the throat and the wingtips. The underside also had two wood-veneer circles, for balance, inlaid with laminated peacock feathers. Kris straddled the back of the creature and prised open the canopy of the cockpit. He slid in beneath the skin, glowing with pleasure. His hands jumped from knob to button; he checked all the instruments and levers. The tail and flaps flickered into life as the strings and rods pulled and pushed, lubricated by their auto-pulse grease nipples.

'It is very pretty,' Jaz admitted, 'but what's this?' He pointed to a rip along the along the edge of the starboard wing. Kris climbed down and examined the tear painstakingly, his fingers touching each damaged ligament, probing, smoothing, already restoring.

'That's torn, isn't it?' Jaz ran his fingers behind his. 'How could you fix that?'

Kris gently rolled back a layer of thin material. 'Dope resin and aluminium paint.'

I noticed a small engine behind a bench at the back of the hangar. I pulled it out.

'Is that the whatsit?' Jaz gasped in disbelief.

'A motor.' Kris nodded at the propellor mounted at the back. 'A very neat little motor for that.' He unfastened the casing and examined the copper coils of an electromagnet.

I asked him how it worked.

'Electricity.' Kris glanced across at Jaz and smiled. All around him the tools of a mechanical enthusiast lay in readiness: long-nose pliers, screwdrivers, grips and vices, clips and cogwheels, wires and fuses. He set to work immediately, reassembling the motor and working out the gearing for the propellor. The whole hangar seemed to hum to his fingers, a prototype to the sound of the motor itself.

'You are not fixing that for us to go in, are you?' Jaz tapped Kris on the shoulder.

Kris looked up briefly, but said nothing.

I told them both about the glimpse I had had of the plains below.

'You are not going to get me in that. It looks cute and I have an awful lot of faith in dear Kris, you know, but I don't think the birdie-bee thing is for me, actually.'

I was tempted to mention the dead bodies buried in the garden, or to remind Jaz of the helicopter above the tea estate.

'Anyway, it's a museum piece. Just a thingamajig for kooky curators to party in. Look, the seats are made out of leather, for God's sake.' Jaz slapped his hands together, done with the discussion. 'If you really want to leave here, you guys better fix the cruiser we came in instead.'

★   ★   ★

By the end of the day Kris had powered up a work bench and was completely absorbed in his laborious repairs. I slipped back into the hangar to observe him. He was working, hunched over a thin opaque solar panel. His black soldering iron rested – like one of Eldon's everpresent cigarettes – on the rim of a saucer, a thin spiral of smoke rising out of its bubbling silver tip. Next to it, the fuse wire and pliers waited, primed. He had also brought out some copper sheeting and a hammer. One sheet was already stippled. I watched, mesmerised, as he picked up the soldering iron and brought its tip to the bare end of a thin red wire pressed against a terminal on the panel. In the silence of the hangar the soft metal sizzled like flesh. He checked the other terminal; satisfied, he carried the panel over and slotted it into place.

I coughed and stepped closer. Kris looked up as though out of another world. 'How is it?' I asked.

He shrugged. 'It'll fly.' He showed me how the power-lines ran through the plane. There was a small battery linked to the solar panels as well as to the electric motor he had fixed behind the cockpit. Watching Kris work on the controls, I wished I had learnt to fly like my father had and his before him. For once there seemed a point to those frequent recourses to waving arms, diagrams of airfoils, leading edges, trailing edges, angles of attack and centres of gravity with which Eldon tried to illustrate the laws of physics to me. But as far as I could tell from Kris's actions, this particular machine had been simplified to the point of virtual automation. I tried to get him to show how each of its minimised controls functioned. He seemed willing to give more than he ever had before. He explained how the aircraft had been designed for power-assisted gliding. His voice was gruff but, for the first time, unstoppable. 'A beautiful machine, so light, so aerodynamic. The solar battery and motor will be very efficient once you are up in the air, but you have to use a catapult like the one outside to get up to speed for the necessary lift. You need a bit of luck. With that massive drop at the cliff-edge, this is probably the only place on the island you can be sure of a flight without being towed.' His voice trailed away. 'It is also the only way out of here.'

I closed my eyes.

'It's a two-seater. When the time comes, one of us will have to stay behind,' he added quietly, reading my mind.

Outside, the night sky swung low. The mountain air as chilly as the cold that numbed me before I ever came here, before I met Uva, as though perhaps she was slowly forgetting me; withdrawing into a world of her own, as she seems to even now. I tried to imagine how we might fly. I saw my father in the sky fighting for his life.

Even after Lee's death, Eldon found it hard to accept that his son had ever decided to fly as a fighter. It was the only thing that made him lose his temper. I would never forget the time some long-lost acquaintance of his had asked, in innocence, 'And Lee? What's the young hero up to now?'

My father had been dead for over a year, but Eldon acted as though he had only just flown away. 'He had a lovely wife. Penny had a very important job, first-class research – your field, in fact. Bio-whatever. They produced a fine son. Marc here. Everything was perfect. And then he just buzzed off.'

'Flyer, no? Artist of gravity, like you.'

'Fellow went like a bloody mercenary . . .'

'Eldon!' Cleo jerked around and glared at her husband.

'Well, what was his business? Another bloody war. And

what for? You think it is for peace? After everyone is destroyed, is that peace? Is that what they got after that débâcle in the desert? What do you think he was going to do this time? Sell ice-cream? It was the same bloody business, I bet you. Gunships with bullets like bombshells. You've seen what they look like. Those are killing machines. For annihilators not aviators . . .' Eldon slammed his fist into the palm of his other hand and stormed out of the room.

My profound aversion to flight was reinforced in the mounting air strikes and perpetual strategic bombardment of those years; like many of my isolated generation, I learnt to tune my screen to entertainment-only channels designed to massage all our surface irritations. Life increasingly became pleasured only by bits. After Cleo died there really seemed nothing left to care for, nothing worthwhile. Nothing until my father reached back through his celluloid wormhole to prompt me to unearth a past of my own; a line that might make sense from one moment to the next, and to find out whether it was better to remember, or better to forget, stuck as we were on this beleaguered world.

That night in Farindola, standing at the edge with my hands in my pockets, I kept wondering whether I was on the verge of something new or something old; whether what I wanted was something behind me, or something ahead.

Inside the hangar a high-pitched whine started. There were several short bursts, and then a long, piercing bout of drilling.

Over the next three days while Jaz cooked and cleaned and preened himself, Kris concentrated on the aircraft. I swung from one to the other with a growing sense of helplessness. They both seemed to have attained some peculiar anodyne state through their respective labours, but I was impatient. I was anxious to move on. To find Uva. On the third evening, as I hurried back from the hangar, I heard an owl hoot. It was the signal she used whenever we met at our rendezvous near her farm. I wondered whether she too had found Farindola first, before Samandia. Stars littered the sky above, but she was nowhere to be seen.

Inside the dining room, when I shut the door, I was back in limbo again.

'Is Kris going to be out there all night?' Jaz complained, as he spooned out another of his lovingly prepared meals. 'Is he going to eat at midnight again? Alone?' Jaz's voice, exasperated as though by a wayward charge, hovered over the dining table suggesting an intimacy of shared responsibility. But I recognised in Kris's devoted attention to the aircraft a kind of obsession. I told Jaz that the aircraft was more or less completely restored.

'So what? Is he going to fly away now?' He fluttered his hands and leant forward, flaring his pampered nostrils to catch the smell of crushed cloves and juniper in what he called his scrummy curry.

'Tomorrow, I guess. With one of us.'

'Why?' He glared at me.

'We can't stay here for ever. The cruiser is no good any more.'

Jaz was silent for a while. I could see tears in his eyes. 'But I'm happy here like this. Maybe fresh air and celibacy do suit me. I don't really want either of us to go anywhere.' Then he rose, snuffling loudly. He crumpled up his serviette and squeezed it in his hands. 'How about a game, Marc. I found a carrom board. You know how to play?'

★   ★   ★

Carrom was my favourite childhood game; I loved the speed and sound of it. I loved flicking my finger to spin the wooden billiard pucks on our polished, sherbet-scented board with its painted mandala and silk pockets. The wooden board, about the size of a card-table, would be brought out by Eldon every Sunday afternoon; he would snap his fingers against the ivory striker like a master player. The clucks, the clicks, the hiss of the pucks flying across the pale wood dusted with Imperial Leather talc were the most precious sound charts of those days before my pop, rock, dub and rap; those days of my growing older as Eldon grew old. 'You are a much better player than your father,' he would declare as though he wished Lee had tried harder to find the romance of spinning and speeding and unerring accuracy on the board, rather than over the deserts and dry lands of his war-zones.

I would watch, fascinated, as Eldon flicked with his fingers: middle to the thumb. On some days they looked thick and swollen, about to burst. On other days they would seem withered, brittle and skeletal. And yet somehow, at the stroke, they would always thrum perfectly and leave his knotted palm wonderfully open in a gesture of pure delight. I'd stare at it and then look up to find Eldon observing me. 'I wish I could see out of your eyes, son: live another lifetime and see what it would be like even thirty years from now.' His son's eyes, and his son's son's eyes, were all that Eldon seemed to wish for in the end, although each day he seemed to play more and more with the shadows of his youth rather than the company now present. Perhaps we all do.

The next day I woke up tense, as though all night I had dreamed of Kris's drill, his spanner and his hammer, screwing, tightening, banging until every single muscle of mine was hinged like an aileron. I went to breakfast in trepidation, trying to sort my concern for Uva from my worries about Kris and his aircraft. Jaz was already up, sipping blossom-tea by the window. Outside the early mist had cleared and the sun was melting on the hills. I filled a large mug with hot water from the urn and brought it over. Jaz looked up, but said nothing.

I asked what was wrong.

'I don't know. I don't feel so good. I woke up with a real headache.' He wrinkled up his nose.

'Drowned your losses with too much gin last night?'

'No, not that kind. More like a bad dream. I even tried to wash it out.' He gave a little shiver to shake it off.

I asked if he'd seen Kris.

'Funny guy, really. I think he still disapproves of me deep down, you know? He really doesn't want to talk to me – to us – does he? Like we are trespassing on his property all the time, don't you think?'

Peering over his bowl of steaming tea, Jaz seemed in that unleavened light more vulnerable than ever. His face was creased like a much older man's, his eyes heavy and marbled, but there was something very delicate about the way he propped his chin on just one curved finger. His whole body seemed to be curling in on itself, the shoulders furled around a collapsed chest, a neglected heart.

'You don't disapprove as well, do you?' He fiddled with his tea-bowl, spinning the blue porcelain landscape of willow trees, birds and pagodas hopelessly in a circle on the table.

'Disapprove of what?'

'Oh, I don't know.' He pushed the bowl away and stood up. He was wearing one of the foil jump suits he had found in the small gym downstairs; he straightened out the wrinkles around his thighs and redid the Velcro straps on the cuffs. His hair was still damp and some of it was caught inside his collar. He freed it and checked his reflection in the window. There was a bit right at the back sticking out. 'A duck's arse, no?' He tried to smooth it down, stroking the back of his head with his ladylike fingers. Then his face brightened. 'But your darling Uva . . . she really knows how to treat me. I do love her, you know, almost as much as you.'

Before I could ask him what exactly he meant, the door to the dining room burst open, splintering the air with flying glass. My blood stopped. A stream of camouflage khaki poured in, filling the room with the stench of soldiers, sweat and gun oil. At first I saw only the glint of cats' eyes, a blur of Maravil uniforms. Jaz collapsed back on to his chair, ashen, his arms like frail sticks on the table. We had only an ivory-handled butter knife between us. Half a dozen soldiers formed a semicircle by the door. The commander was a small wolfish man in a cap. He screamed out, 'Up against the glass, gollas.' But before I could get to my feet, the gun in his hand fired. Jaz's bowl exploded in front of him and the hot brew scalded him. A thin shard of china nicked a pink groove across his face. He recoiled, jumping back, toppling his chair, but he didn't make a sound. The cut on his smooth cheek turned bright crimson. 'Up, up, up,' the commander shrieked. His tongue was stained black like the gums of his teeth. The whole face disfigured by a life too long at war with itself. He fired again, expertly, and the bullet grazed the table top close to my fingers. 'Up, up.' I pressed back against the glass wall. The commander crowed: his pack stood fast, feet apart, mouths pinched, guns to the ready.

I felt hollow and impotent before the fury. Nothing in my body seemed to work; the whole room rocked out of focus.

He strode up to Jaz and prodded his gun hard into Jaz's navel. He traced a line up to his throat and stuck the barrel under Jaz's chin. When Jaz lifted his head up, the commander grabbed the thong on his zipper and pulled. The front of the jump suit ripped open. He screamed out another order. Jaz looked helplessly at me, unable to talk, his charm torn out of him. For a moment he looked about to cry, but he screwed his eyes tight and peeled off the rest of his suit. His clenched, quivering stomach already bore the mark of the gun barrel. The man then thrust the gun into Jaz's groin and barked until his shrill voice skidded off every wall. Jaz's exposed genitals shrank to a tiny nubble. I was sure the gun would fire again; explode the flesh flattened against it.

Instead he pulled back and snapped at one of his men. The soldier marched out and a moment later returned pushing a cowed figure in front of him. As he stumbled towards us, my last hopes sank. Somehow, at the back of my mind, I had hoped Kris might save us yet.

'These?' the commander snarled.

Kris's head was bowed low. 'Yes, Captain,' he spluttered. Then he looked up at me briefly, his eyes drowning. They had broken his nose. His mouth had blood smeared around it. There were burns on his neck.

I turned to Jaz, confused. But before he could respond, the commander shoved Kris to one side and grabbed Jaz. 'You, puckface, run to jungle, now. Wanna hunt, hunt, hunt.' He pushed him and turned to me. 'You tourfucker, you gonna die here.' I could see the lard turn to sweat around his mouth; his cat's eye numbed me.

Then, as he raised his gun, Jaz hurled himself forward, howling. They both toppled to the ground. The gun went off in a burst of blood. Jaz got hold of the gun and, using the commander's twitching body as a shield, fired at the rest of the squad who were too astonished by his actions to react. Two soldiers fell immediately under his fusillade; the others dived for cover behind tables and chairs. Jaz swung around and fired at the glass wall behind me, shattering it. He kept firing, spraying the rest of the room. 'Go, darling, go,' he yelled at me before a burst of gunfire ripped his human shield from him. I saw his tender, graceful throat perforate, his huge lips seeming still to mouth silently even as his blood pumped out of the sudden black wounds. More bullets ploughed into his body, puncturing the skin and bursting open his bare breast, snapping rib after rib, pulverising the vertebra of his arched column. Another gun fired. Kris, from the floor, killed the remaining three soldiers within seconds. Kris's front was soaked in blood. One of his legs was riddled; the kneecap was smashed and showed bits of white bone. The leg squeaked, dangling behind him, as he shifted his position to reach over Jaz's hewn, rented body and pull at the commander's belt of bombs and bullets. I heard a groan as the body rolled over. I couldn't speak. My ears were ringing. Then another bunch of soldiers tried to storm the room. Guns thundered. Kris fired back with one hand while with the other he released a grenade from the thick canvas belt. His face was all screwed up. 'Jump,' he yelled at me under the barrage. Then he bit the detonator pin and pulled it out with his teeth. I watched him count to five. '*Now.*' He kept the grenade gripped in his hand.

I rolled back and jumped out of the hole in the glass wall. The blast seemed to push me out on to the soft slopes of the lower garden.

There was a succession of explosions set off by Kris's: the whole building shook. As the debris – fragments of old ochre tile, furniture, cinders – rained down around me, I headed out into the reserve, towards the cliff. Behind me I could hear the commotion of more soldiers in what remained of the building.

When I reached the landing strip I was shaking. I could see the doors of Kris's workshop had been rolled back and, right next to it, out in the open, the aircraft hitched on to the catapult, its arced wings quivering in the light wind, more like a butterfly's than a peacock's.

It looked ready to fly. I saw Kris's ghost making his final checks. I hesitated, but there was no choice; I had to trust in what was before me.

I climbed up into the feather-trimmed cockpit forcing myself to recall the sequence of actions Kris had mimed for me. I strapped myself in. There was a din growing under the trees. I could hear vehicles racing and soldiers shouting. Holding my breath, I whispered a little prayer while my fingers searched for the small red starter button; when I found it, I immediately pressed it. The wooden propellor whirred: *Kris. Kris. Kris.* I shut my eyes and released the catch of the catapult. The chain rattled out and there was a jolt as the aircraft trundled the first few metres. I urged it, 'Move.' It yawed and my insides heaved, turning over. Then the mechanism underneath clunked into place and the aircraft hurtled forward. I felt the wind rush through a small passage in its throat as the great wooden bird finally took to the air.

V

THE GARDEN

H OURS LATER my whole body seemed to rock with the flow of blood; a gentle movement allied to the rise and fall of soft sifted breath in deep flesh. Numbness had spread from one leg up through my shoulders into the lower part of my head. There was comfort in the heavy smell of warm water, the fecundity of low-lying leaves, steaming chlorophyll, and hot moist air raddled with pollen. A light lapping vibrated through the wood with occasional clicks and chuckles as the rudder swung, or a flap slapped the water like a sucked flipper. Splintered sunbeams illuminated the cracks in the faciaboard, spiralling wood-motes and the floating debris of brushed feather dust. I unbuckled the strap that held me and the blue webbing retracted lazily, as though the coil had to remember what needed to be done warp by weft. I straightened up, shifting my weight from one side to the other. Everything rolled alarmingly. I saw that the plane was floating on a lake filled with lotuses and water hyacinth. The nearest shore was about a forty metres away and thick with lowland trees. My leg wouldn't move. There was no wound to be seen; no pain. But slowly, as it revived, blood seemed to bruise the flesh. I slid back the glass dome of the cockpit; the air outside was dank, sweet, dense. There was no sound except for the lapping of the water against the fuselage, and round flat leaves flopping. The lily pads were familiar. Like those in the Waterlily House in Kew. I closed my eyes and remembered one time when we had all gathered together outside the entrance: Eldon, Cleo, my father and my mother. My father took me by the hand and pulled me towards the steamed-up door. But Eldon didn't want us to go in. 'It's too hot in there. The Palm House is better.'

My father glowered back at Eldon. 'You used to say this was more like the place where you were born.'

Eldon looked surprised, although I imagine he must have felt a tinge of secret pleasure.

Before they could argue, Grandma Cleo intervened. 'Did you hear the peacock? Down by the lake? I'll take the little one to see it. Penny, you come too.'

I can never forget the disappointment when my father let go of my hand and disappeared into the Waterlily House alone. I did not have the words to say what I felt then; I could only look. My grandfather wagged his head gloomily and ambled towards the large glass Palm House opposite instead.

Cleo and my mother started towards the lake, but I refused to budge. I wanted to wait for my father. When he finally came out Cleo told him, 'This little one wouldn't move without you. He wants us all to stay together.'

I did.

When I forced open my eyes again, I expected to see them all by my bed. Instead I found only the jungle frowning around a giant eye. A little unsteadily, I stepped out on to the wing. I lay down, spread-eagled, and sipped a handful of silky water. Only then did I try to get the aircraft to move, paddling without much effect. I climbed back into the cockpit and tested the rudder pedals; they were still wired up. I worked them, slowly wagging the tail-fin from side to side. Part of it was submerged in the water and as a result the plane nosed forward. I pushed harder, right and left, right and left. The big bird began to waddle towards the shore like some slow beast from the past.

When I released the catch on the catapult, seconds before the soldiers stormed the airstrip, my hands had automatically gone to the joystick, my feet instinctively to the rudder bar. I had to forget the terror of the troops, Jaz's breached body, the detonation of the grenade exploding in Kris's hand. Somehow I had to learn to fly. I felt the control stick drag as the plane and the wind pressed against each other. I held it firm and the aircraft soared. The whistling of the cold air, the spinning propellor and the emptiness of the sky above the clouds soon soothed me as the wings caught the updraught of a sea-thermal rising against the mountains. The altimeter needle spun faster. The plane climbed higher. The piece of red yarn taped to the outside of the glass flew safe and straight in the airstream. I levelled off up there like an ace. My father would have been proud of me.

The plane floated free for ages until Farindola, wreathed in smoke far behind, seemed no longer even to exist. Then the horror of it all caught up with me and I lost control. The motor cut out: my peacock dipped. The electric starter would not fire again. I didn't panic: methodically I tested the controls and managed to bring the plane to an even, steady descent. In the distance, to my right, I could see a solitary mountain; below me the spiky canopy of a rainforest; and not too far away the moist alluring eye I had been looking for. The beaked head below me seemed to crane forward.

If not for the smooth upward curve of its neck, the landing would have been a dive. The bang was hard but before my head struck the sidebar, I saw the water rise in a huge spray around the cockpit as the plane gouged the lake.

Once I got ashore, I felt I had to rest. I needed more strength to explore. As the light began to fail, water sounds grew: a steady lapping, the plopping of what could have been fish breaking the surface. Insects whirling in the twilight.

I ate a chewbar from the survival kit and watched the water like a hunter, as Kris would have. Should have? The evening air was warm. My whole body was warm: skin, blood, porous flesh. If Jaz was there, he'd have been bustling about: washing, flossing, preparing himself for the night, chatting, honking and gabbing; sucking in his cheeks, rolling his eyes and talking non-stop to keep the darkness at bay. How I wished I could. Despite what had happened, I found I could think of him quite calmly. It was as though by flying I had been able to leave my emotions behind. Up in the sky a magnified moon appeared, staining the world with false light.

In the morning, I remembered that if this was the region where Eldon had described small coconut estates floating like oases in the jungle, then there should be some sign of human habitation around. It was somewhere here, long before the bombing, the blight and the reasserted jungle, that his beloved twenty acres had once flowered with its thatched cottage and sandy garden: an integral part of my imagination even before Uva made it my promised land.

It didn't take long to reach the first plantation of tall grey trees. They still grew in rows, laced with sunlight. Although not as straight as they once might have stood, they were in better shape than those by the old beach hotel. The ground in between was covered with papery creepers. I stripped a fallen palm frond and cleared a path marking, as I went, a wake which I could follow back later. The older trees looked neglected, but I saw that there were enough nuts around from the younger, wilder ones to feed on as long as I found a way to husk them.

Eventually, I reached a fence: the strands of barbed wire were broken but the concrete posts had survived. On the other side scrub had spread over parts of a road.

I went along it until I arrived at a gateway guarded by two concrete elephant heads. The intertwined arms of an avenue of blossom trees beyond them seemed to beckon me. Their broad rubbery leaves clutched bursts of firm flowers, reds in the first trees, giving way to smooth whites further on; each flower glowed with a rich flame at the centre where the petals retreated in a swirl. I was drawn in. The road then banked around a thick hedge and brought me to the brink of a cry.

The house sat low, dappled in dreamlight. The thatched roof bearing down to the ground in the way stone-age dwellings do – close to the earth – sweeping down like a brushstroke with gaping holes where meteorites could easily have passed through. The wall facing me was a hushed pale yellow, while all around overgrown flowering shrubs had entangled themselves with each other in a cacophony of vaulting purples and oranges. On the left I could see a large empty swimming pool, with dwarf palms and lime trees dotted around it in the sand. Beyond the main house, like playground shelters, several smaller mud huts and sheds languished in various stages of disrepair.

I knew then that this had to be the place I had always been yearning for without ever quite knowing it; but was it my refuge or a place already occupied? Although the house looked neglected, the exuberant flowers gave the place an air of continuing habitation. I knew I should be cautious. I slipped back behind the hedge and settled down as though it were a nest that needed to be watched. My nerves were bare. I felt drained.

I wondered whether my father might be inside, not dead but another recluse hiding out in an ancestral home, waiting for things to turn better, a son to find his true self. Lee, the ancient aviator threading seashells, waiting to be relieved of his story; his blue-winged Kfir, dripping wax, tucked away in a thatched hangar. If he were to emerge, I wondered, what should I say?

'It's me. Marc. The son you left behind.' The words tightened into a child's fist. 'I've come, like you wanted me to.' Yes, I would have asked him. 'So what was it that brought you here, Papa? That has kept you here? Where was the wedding? What happened to the band?'

I saw him as an old man, now more like Eldon than anyone else; a strong gaunt face, a mantle of silver hair. His phantom voice would be gravelly. *'I came, son, because I love this place. The warm ocean breeze, the smell of the earth here, the closeness of the moon. When my father first brought me here, I realised this was what I had been looking for all my life. From the first moment I saw the curve of its vulnerable coastline, as we flew in, I knew I would one day have to make this place my own. Just breathe this air, feel the texture of the jasmine, the lantana, the lilies. This was a garden like I had never imagined before. Have you seen the parrots? The orioles? The woodpeckers? The sky is magic. More full of stars than I had ever dreamt of before. I fell in love here. I wasn't leaving you when I returned here. I came because I knew that one day you would too, and I had to do the best I could to preserve something of what I found here for you.'*

'But you came because of war, a destroyer . . .' Eldon's distraught accusation echoed in my head.

'No, son. I came to save what I found here, before it was all squandered away. I came to do what I believed was right.'

I imagined him, in his youth, arguing with his own father as they drove around the hills of this island. *'No, they must not flood the valleys, the old tanks will do. No, they must not destroy the forests, these animals must live too. No, no more plantations of tea. Go for bio-diversity. No, no more history. No more insane bloody foolery. No more war to end war.'*

My eyes were smarting. I was completely disoriented. You can't do that, I wanted to retaliate. But it was my grandfather, surely, not my father speaking. The garden could only be his. This had to be the cottage he was so fond of, the one he had searched for in vain with his son. That was a kingfisher, not a Kfir.

No one emerged. *A voyage of love.* I realised I was delirious. If anyone would have been hiding inside, it would have been Uva, not my sparring paternal ghosts. Uva, I whispered to myself, with her feathers unfolding.

Yet, I felt more like a child stirring there, than a lover.

A mosaic path glittered under a film of sand. It snaked between large earthenware pots and concrete urns up to a patio sheltered by a luscious pergola of rumpled leaves and white trumpet flowers. A small veranda led to the house itself where big brown shutters sealed the doorway like the flaps of a storybook.

I moved forward slowly, bathed in sweat.

Under the pergola the patio had been tiled in cobalt; the

chipped metal chairs and tables, even the light that entered, was cool.

On the other side paving stones led across the sand to a wooden door blocked by a fallen branch. The house must have been abandoned. I breathed a little easier and edged forward as though into an adventure film from a golden era.

The door creaked open. I could make out a big stone sink in one corner and a long galley of waxed cupboards. I poked my stick into the room and rapped the walls: *tak, tak, tak*. Nothing flew out. No bats, rats or night owls. Not the slightest rustle of life. Even the roaches must have left, I thought. The sink was dry. Above a ledge thin strips of light outlined a closed window. I opened it. Bright sun lit a table piled with clay pots and utensils. A child's shrunken football was lodged underneath, just as mine used to end up under the work bench in Eldon's garage. In the still warm air I heard Jaz's haunting exclamations as he uncovered the cornucopia of our Farindola larder. If only he were here . . . It hurts to remember everything that has happened, but at least here, with my eyes closed, I find it easier to mould memory to need and practise the simplest art of survival.

In the centre of the house there was enough light from a small spiral staircase to see a cane settee, a dresser and two wooden trunks. In a corner, a small glass-fronted case held some old almanacs and magazines. There was a yellowed newspaper clipping tacked to the side: a picture of a small padded batsman leaping up, both feet off the ground, hitting a cricket ball high into the sky.

The big trunks were like treasure chests: packed with sheets, towels, sarongs, cotton quilts. To me they all seemed pristine despite being threadbare.

The orderliness with which everything had been packed

away, except for the football, suggested a house that was never permanently occupied. Every item was storable, kept for periodic not constant use. The place had not been abandoned in a hurry; the family it belonged to seemed to have closed up the house at the end of one weekend, and gone away never to come back.

Some people are able to do that, I guess; perhaps have to do that: close the door and never look back, never return. Perhaps it is what everyone wants to do. After Eldon died, I remember his old friend Anton's refrain: 'Leave the past behind, Cleo. Pack your bags. I'll help you move somewhere new.' But she wouldn't. She said she wanted to stay while Eldon's beloved roses continued to bloom, and she still had the strength to tend to their neat suburban beds.

Exploring the house I felt I too might be able to keep some faith here.

There were two rooms, one on either side of the stairway, each with two beds. The smaller one, stencilled with birds and fish, had a toy cupboard crammed full of jigsaws, board games and crumpled inflatables for the pool. It felt safe despite what had happened to the rest of the region. Perhaps Samandia was the preserve of the gods. I was ready to believe it.

The upper floor turned out to be a large open arena where the slanted roof had been extended to form the only wall. The other sides were shielded by nylon tats which dropped below the edge of a wooden balustrade. From the front I could see a riot of pinks and oranges. Colours that seemed profoundly familiar. Beyond the flowers, where the sand gave way to tough wild grass, coconut palms reached up towards the sky, and beyond them tall jungle trees sprouted small red flames. Just to look at the jumble of blossom, the shimmering herringbone fronds, was to revel in life that seemed amaranthine. I could live here, I told myself then as Jaz might have. There was even an enclosed crop garden and several fruit trees, including mango.

As I surveyed my new domain two ring-neck parakeets screeched past, their short wings furiously beating the warm thick air. They shot between the trees – fast, hard, green bullets – and headed towards the lake I had come from. Their screeches echoed the glee of similar parakeets arriving in Eldon's garden one summer. I had been the first to notice the new migrants on the Victoria plum tree that spread its long, arching branches over the rose bushes. There were three of them, startlingly green, seeming to climb out of my jungle book then, ripping into the soft mildewed fruit with their bright red beaks. I dragged Eldon out to look at them because the old man had not believed me. 'There are no parakeets in this country, my dear boy.' But I was right; they were parakeets, and they thrived in his garden, the botanical gardens nearby, and all the fruit orchards of southern England, adding vivid colours, loud songs and unexpected eating habits to the jetscuffed end of his brittle British century.

Marooned on this hallucinogenic island, I felt I had finally reached the original home of those chance migrants and the other brightly coloured birds that had fascinated me all my boyhood. I was convinced that this, not the Palm Beach coast, was my actual haven – my real destination. Hers and mine.

In a storeroom I discovered mattresses wrapped in plastic, charcoal, paraffin, candles, a carton of matchboxes and a case of arrack. Right at the back a vintage rifle, protected by an oilcloth, and a box of bullets. The rifle had a brass name-plate pinned to its wooden stock: Lee-Enfield. I was delighted.

I wanted to explore the other sheds and huts to see what else I might recognise, but I was ravenous by then. From the walled enclosure I collected a gourd, some okra, various wild fruit and a handful of speckled beans and brought them back to the house. The flesh of the gourd was hard and needed to be boiled. Using some twigs from the garden I set about making a fire in the stone stove outside. It took several attempts. Eldon would have been appalled: 'You must learn the basics of survival. How to make a fire, walk without water, control your sphincter. You have to be prepared for anything, my boy, and be completely self-sufficient.' I remembered him telling me how on their famous trip together, he and Lee had trekked for hours through the last remaining rainforest of the island in search of a smoking waterfall and a leopard without spots. 'I couldn't keep up,' Eldon confessed stifling a guffaw. 'Your father could trek all day without even stopping for a pee. He learned to survive, you see, on nothing but his wits and a bit of self-control.'

Finally I had discovered, it was exactly what I needed to learn too.

That night, watching the candlelight, I couldn't stop the final images of Jaz and Kris from returning. I tried to recall our earlier moments together instead. Especially Jaz presenting his elegant vegetarian dishes, chatting in his easy way, wheedling persistently whenever his curiosity was aroused; giving the few precious days we had in Farindola a rare charm.

I remembered how one evening he had flourished a kitchen knife and done his little Torvill dance, using a tea-towel as a mask. 'Look at this. It's so sharp you could split a lentil with it.'

Something in the way he held it spun me back.

'What's wrong?'

'Nothing. You just remind me of someone.'

'A real devil?'

'My mother, actually,' I blurted out.

His eyes widened, tickled by the thought. 'Really. Tell me about her. What was she like? I bet she was gorgeous.'

'It's just the knife you were waving about. I remember her with a knife.' A fragment of a memory from the last time I had seen my mother and my father together surfaced.

'Like Uva's?' Jaz asked surprised.

'No.' I shook my head. 'No, it was a kitchen knife. Like that one. She had it in her hand.' My father was back from one of his journeys abroad. My mother was in the kitchen.

'What did she do?' Jaz asked.

I didn't know. I still don't know. 'That is all I remember,' I said. 'He left after that, I think. He came here for ever.'

'Why?'

I had asked my grandmother Cleo the same question when I was older. Why did he leave? Why did he never come back? Was there an argument? I remember Cleo placing her hand over mine and speaking in a slightly husky voice. 'You see, my dear, Lee was always fascinated by the prospect of adventure. That's why he joined the RAF. The uniform seemed so much more glamorous to him than your grandfather's flying school kit. And Lee so loved those fast fighter planes. He wanted to go faster, you know, than his dad in his little Cessna. Faster and further. But after that Gulf effort, he said he needed to believe in something that made more sense. He seemed to think his father's old home could give him that. I told him life grows from the inside, but I guess we all need a little prompting to start us off. He spent a whole year on the island. He met your mother there. He fell in love and wanted to make it their home one day. So a few years later, when he was asked if he would go back and do some work there, he felt he couldn't refuse. I think they needed someone to help with air supplies for refugees, or something, but Eldon could never believe that the plane he was in that day was not military. He wouldn't listen to anyone. Not even me. He never forgave Lee for getting into a uniform in the first place. But I'm sure Lee wanted to show us what else he could do. You see, your father always thought he could do everything, handle anything. He wasn't really leaving you, or your mother, you know. He went because he believed he was needed there. He always said he was just going ahead, to sort a few things out. He wanted us all to be able to join him one day.'

If only that was true. If only there was a place where we would be reunited for ever with the ones that we lose. If only this was such a place. Perhaps it is. Perhaps that is what the earth is. Our world. A place where we look for those we had lost elsewhere in our previous, less evolved, lives. Could it be? But I have found nothing of his actual life here, or of any of those whom I have missed.

I didn't want to dwell on him any more that night. I thought I would try to settle down in the smaller bedroom – the child's room. The sky was visible through the window in there. I lay down looking out for the stars I knew must still be sparking somewhere. I fell asleep dreaming of fathers again; this time not mine.

★   ★   ★

I dreamed of a big man, sturdily built, with a large broad chest and an impressive mane of thick black hair. He wore an orange sarong and a copper armband. He carried a scythe with one hand and held a bronze spear in the other. He was standing barefoot on a beach. At his feet a peacock struggled with a silver arrow in its throat. The sky was pitch-black and there was water, impending water, everywhere. He spoke, but his words were in a language I did not understand. He knelt down and tried to remove the arrow from the bird. The arrowhead was caught in the cords of its throat. Each time he pulled the shaft, the bird would rise trying to cry but the only sound came from its flapping feathers. Beneath them the barbed wings of a steel warplane glinted. He put his foot on the bird's thin blue neck and yanked the arrow once more. The moment it came out, another arrow rushed through the air. This one pierced his own throat. Both arrows looked as though they had once belonged in his leather quiver. As he fell, he seemed to change shape into a leopard. I heard Uva cry out, calling him father. I looked around and saw her bathing in a stream. She had a cloth wrapped around her and knotted above her breasts. The cloth was wet and clung to her skin. With each bowlful of water that she poured, she seemed to dissolve. I shouted out to her but my voice couldn't reach her. The air thickened with a curtain of rain between us. The river-bank I stood on began to erode. The dotted pattern in the cloth washed away, then the cloth itself melted, leaving her naked in the brief light before her figure too went. The rain, like the waters of the river, turned red; a familiar contaminated waterhole-red. I kept calling to her. I could hear her murmuring; I floated on the contours of the sound. From the shore I entered my cell in the compound outside Maravil and tripped over a polythene bag. Inside it were her remains: a silk skin. In my ear her voice echoed singing the praises of a cocoon.

'Where are you?' I shouted, knowing that her presence could not have been only in that discarded shape. Her life was not just breath, but an incarnation surely of a soul wishing; wishing still to share our temporary illumination.

I heard her cry out again. The sound woke me.

I was in a sweat: my face and hands had been bitten all over. Warnings about maladies and fatal infections, the rows upon rows of repellents and prophylactics I had ignored at the chemist back at the terminal before I set off, whizzed around mocking me. My arms ached; my head was swollen. The insides of my thighs hurt. All my muscles seemed to have been twisted in the night. As I tried to unstretch, the sole of my left foot curled in a spasm. It was unbearable. I wanted to pull it apart; turn my body inside out and tear it to shreds. My skin was burning, itching, retreating. I flung off the sheet and saw my body had erupted. I tried to bend my toes but they were like stumps. I could see horns protruding, yellowed and ridged. My bones being extruded. The journey from life to death, I realised then, was an unpeeling. The converting of an inner life into an outer.

Where was the boatman who stripped back the layers?

I felt sure Uva was dead. I wanted to plunge into her darkest, thickest jungle to die too and rot; fertilise her wretched earth if nothing else.

Then an excruciating, gut-wrenching cramp wrung every tube in the pit of my body. I wanted to scream to do something to ease the pain.

I staggered out of the house into the trees, trying to keep moving. As I blundered about the jungle, punching at leaves, the sounds that had plagued me slowly receded, the gripe eased. But even there it seemed Eldon had to have the last word. I don't know why, or how, he came to be the arbiter of my whole life. I couldn't stop him. 'We all have a vision of the world as it should be, and our place in it.' He launched into another of his little sermons. 'But for most of us it takes a lifetime to discover it.' Good, I was exhausted. My life was over. I wanted no more of his dodgy homilies. I wanted everything to be over. There seemed no point in drawing it out. Stop breathing, I told myself, and soon it would end. But then, a little further on, I heard the sound of another breath: a lung exhaling, inhaling. Slow, deliberate, difficult breathing. There was nothing to be seen that could be making the sound until, in a clump of overgrown roots, I spied a small brown huddle. A foot clawed the air as if trying to get a hold of something to push it further into the centre. The creature tired quickly and lay with its eyes half closed. I made a soothing, clucking sound and pushed some leaves towards it. There was no reaction. I touched it. The fur was warm. It still did not react. I thought it must have died, sapped by its last effort to escape, and touched it again, feeling warm meat underneath. This time it did move, revealing a wound on its arm. I tried to shift the awkward limb and the monkey whimpered. It is sometimes kinder to kill, I remembered.

I couldn't. I felt a bond. Evolution was not the survival of the fittest. Our evolution must come from the survival of the weak, retrieved against the odds, I realised. It must matter, otherwise why would we care about anyone? How could I have felt anything meaningful for Uva, if we were only the random firing of some scattered neurones; the accidental binding of chemicals in a pointless law of cosmic efficiency? I could see then why I had to value life over death. Any life, including mine.

I couldn't live without Uva, but if I was to die without her, I would have to come back and start again. Samandia was the only safe place I knew she knew. We have to live in hope. It was clear to me then that I had to help the animal to survive. I stripped off my shirt to use as a sack to carry it. Only when I lifted the creature up did I notice one of its legs was also hurt. It was not going to be easy.

Back at the house I cleaned the wounds with lime and gunpowder extracted from a cartridge. I even made a cradle for it out of coconut fronds.

The monkey was too feeble to do anything. I gave it water, and tried to feed it fruit.

'You'll waste away,' I said when it refused to eat, idiotically pleased to be able to address another even with this dire warning, even if it had no understanding of my words. I had made my choice.

Although I still felt a little ill, by evening I was able to coax a small banana into the monkey's mouth. It seemed grateful, and I felt grateful myself for its presence, its vulnerability.

With the monkey dependent on me, my priorities became clear. I thought we would both sleep better on the upper floor where the air was fresher. In a cupboard I found a set of mosquito nets and I rigged one up from a roof beam. I lugged up a mattress for me and a basket for the monkey. It was like becoming a child again, when novelty could so easily displace anxiety.

I felt safer on a solid floor that had escaped the tug of the earth. I wanted to defy the earth. To live with the weightiest things floating above the ground: to bring boulders and rocks, a bathful of water, tubs of flowering shrubs, a garden plot, anything and everything upstairs. All to float in a world above a world. To live in the gracious memory of our antenatal flights; our seeking of natural light.

The next morning, rested and collected, I could see a whole day's work fall into place. How I would have to stamp my own mark on the house, shape it to my needs. I felt I should redesign the whole place, become an inventor, an artist and a carpenter. Become my own Kris – even a Crusoe: plunder the wreck, explore the surroundings. There could be other houses around, possibly even inhabited. I felt an urgent need to know more, and to be in control once again. I felt a strength I had not felt before.

The path I had first cut from the lake was still plain to see. Perhaps too plain. Fortunately fresh leaves were beginning to unfurl at the edges, and in the bare patches new life had emerged: oddly shaped black beetles, a line of tottering leaf-cutters, corrugated caterpillars. I picked my way warily around the edge of the lake in case it had already become a trap, but there was nothing to fear.

Pulling the half-beached aircraft right out of the water, I saw again how painstakingly Kris had installed the two solar panels on the wings using bright brass hexagonal screws, how he had replaced the rubber wheels on the fuselage and renovated the padding in the cockpit. It was not so long ago, but already these were the very things that needed to be removed. To be utilitarian – to recycle, to waste not – seemed undeniably right, and yet required a measure of ruthlessness which seemed mercenary. I had to look at everything in that way; those were the values I needed to survive. Need now for ever.

Then, just before I closed up the cockpit, I saw a small parcel lodged between the seat and the safety harness; a piece of silk tied around it.

I had to force the lump in my throat down, hard. Picking up the parcel I slowly unwrapped it.

My first thought was that this time the knife really was Uva's. But again her symbol was not on it. It had to be Kris's. He must have died without it. It floated in my hand, a pair of furled wings. A gift? I climbed out of the aircraft and, once on the ground, flicked it open the way I remembered Kris, and Uva before him, do; like an eye flashing. I stared at it as though by looking I could decipher all its secrets, return all the blood it had let: to the soldier in his workshop, to the bats in the cave, to the old couple in Farindola. By the water's edge I knelt and rinsed the blade. Closing it firmly I placed it in my breast pocket and felt an echo of Uva's hand on it, as though she had reached through the skin of another to touch me again. Warm and close. She would want me to be a survivor; she'd be relying on me to be here. This time I knew I must.

Within a few days I managed to fix the pantry door, refit the pulleys for the broken tat, clear the drains and even re-hang the metal gates, buckled as they were, discovering practical skills I never knew I had. I went back to the aircraft and completely dismantled it. Every mechanical bit, every scrap of wire, wood, strut and bar that might come in useful, I brought back to the sheds around the house and stacked up in a stupendous jigsaw puzzle never to be reconstructed. I made birdhouses to entice barbets, the way Eldon did for his robins and finches, and feeding trays and birdbaths. 'My father must have been the robin,' I quipped to my speechless companion as work displaced despair. 'And I am the son.'

Engrossed in these functional tasks, I didn't worry about what might lie ahead. There had been no sign of any other inhabitants; no sign of any danger. All I was concerned with was to make this place my home and hers: a magnet for our endangered souls.

When the monkey grew strong enough to move I let it wander about the garden. It never wanted to stray very far. It limped about, mimicking me by collecting firewood, bunches of beans, brinjals and bananas.

It wasn't long before I felt the need to tackle the walled crop garden and bring it under proper control too. There was so much I could have learnt from my grandfather about gardening, but all I could recall then was the old man's enthusiasm for watering and for pruning.

'These green suckers have to be taken out,' Eldon used to say, carefully parting the roses. 'Otherwise the whole bush turns to jungle.' As a child I would watch him open his red secateurs and clip the bright new shoots bristling with giant thorns and chuck them to the side of the lawn. 'You see, my boy, you have to look after the old if you want to foster the young.'

He was so proud of his rose garden. He had about two dozen rose bushes: Nymphenburgs, Nur Mahals, Golden Wings and Moonbeams. He was not an expert, but he enjoyed his flowers and tended them with real care. Every month, and sometimes even more frequently, he would visit Kew Gardens to check how well his roses were doing in comparison with those propagated by the professionals. He would pick up tips from the rose beds by the Palm House and marvel at the regimental discipline and unwavering control displayed there. I remember the year he managed to beat the pros for the first bloom. He had celebrated with a chilled bottle of Cava from his local wine shop, where he couldn't stop himself from mentioning it to the young sales assistant. I was with him, choosing a packet of crisps for my treat. 'The bloom,' he had said raising the bottle. 'For the bloom.'

For him the passage of time was marked in a hundred different ways: by plants that blossomed perennially, biannually, diurnally, bushes that fixed the seasons, buds that breathed by the week, the day, the hour, and over them all every few minutes aircraft, kin to his own, that would swing like the carriages of a galactic wheel. He had been a pilot training pilots for most of his life, and a gardener for only his last years. Every four minutes, then every three, and sometimes every two minutes, the roar of a passing aircraft brought back to him his lifelong involvement with the sky, just as each bud in the garden drew him down again to his abiding earth.

'The future,' he was fond of saying, 'is not something you can imagine. You can only rearrange the past in your mind, you know, to look like it is still to come. We have to bathe in a pool of memory, and play little tricks with its surface, just to live another day. We think we are going forwards, but really we are always on a journey going back to find something that we might once almost have had.'

Thinking of my own future, I set about locating the cinnamon and the turmeric that I was sure were growing somewhere around. I found chilli and tomato. I needed more nourishment. I cleared an area bigger than the whole of Eldon's old garden and squeezed seeds wherever I could. I wanted to tame the plot to produce all that I needed, and exactly when I needed it, as ambitious agriculturists the world over have done so often before. All that was required, I believed, was time and keen observation: measurement and calculation, skills I reckoned I must surely have inherited from my fastidious forebears.

By the end of the day I was exhausted; my hands were sore from digging and my skin stung, but I could see I had made a real impression on my surroundings: the ploughed land exuded a sense of real vigour from those wilful acts of ownership. The wilderness was in retreat, but even Uva could only commend me on the flowering it was bound to leave in its wake.

In the days that followed, I became obsessed: planting, replanting, transplanting. I cut an irrigation channel from the well so that even the runoff from my daily wash-bucket ended up watering the crops. I became expert in recognising subtle variations in the podzolic soil. I uncovered a store of rock phosphate in a shed and worked out how to use coconut husks for moisture retention, fibre as mulch, recycle waste through organic compost-generation. I dreamt of domesticating the jungle fowl I had seen running around the lake. I made traps and plans for extensive re-fencing, bringing more and more of the land under my care.

Occasionally I came across useless huts and only once another house of a more substantial nature. I immediately stripped it of fire-lighters and stores. The whole area had been completely depopulated, but it didn't dishearten me. I wrote my initial wherever I went, convinced that one day Uva would come and see my mark and know that I was here, faithfully waiting. With Kris's knife I carved the letter like a bush-lark's wings on tree trunks, I drew it with charcoal and even wrote it in the sand.

During the nights, though, doubts did return. How would she know I'd escaped? She might have thought that, even if I had, I would never make it this far. Maybe I had been too slow in getting to Samandia, just as I had been too slow to save her at our Palm Beach Hotel. The odds were against us there. I should have realised it. The odds were against us all along.

In daylight I didn't let such thoughts deflect me from turning the whole plantation into a self-sustaining refuge. A garden husbanded for her: full of flowering bushes, arboreal vines, thick yellow-bordered, succulent leaves. I embedded red crabclaws in between and arranged bursts of blue tumefied lances in the pots.

Working with the trails of pink and orange and purple that wafted in the warm breeze like butterflies nourished me; those translucent wings gave me a pleasure unlike any of the more utilitarian tasks I had done earlier. Sometimes I would see Jaz in the lazy lift of a dazzling arm, or catch Uva's moist perfume in the cracks between the petals.

I wanted space and order, light and colour. I wanted the place teeming with a hundred different types of birds, of bees, of squirrels. I wanted them all to come, drawn by a lodestone of passion and the heady, overpowering scent of a garden in the middle of a jungle; to bring Uva with them, and if she could not come here, I wanted the garden to become her.

*　　*　　*

Each day I cut a notch on a tree by the well; each night I worked on a crude map using an old table-top and ink made out of charcoal and water.

I dreamt of building a cistern, with an intricate network of bamboo aqueducts hovering just above ground level, perfectly pitched to achieve an overall gradient of a few centimetres. I wanted a smooth even flow which, with little valves and contraflow switches, would measure out the right douche for every one of my favourite plants. I imagined opening the watergate, like an olden-day rajah, as the sun collapsed releasing a perfect benevolent flood. The small electric motor from the aircraft would have been ideal for pumping up the water from the well, except that I couldn't get it to work. I fantasised about harnessing a team of wild oxen to an Archimedean screw, but the practical solution I finally came up with was a windmill to power the spindle on the well.

I designed a set of four sails out of palm fronds and bed linen. I made them to fit the broken propellor from the plane, planning to fix the whole thing to the coconut tree by the well. Only when all the components were in place, on the ground, did I realise that I hadn't worked out how I would get it up high enough. I was furious with myself. While I vented my frustration, the monkey scuttled away to the breadfruit tree at the end of the garden. But my luck held, it seemed then, once again. What was it the old man used to say? 'The difference between the impossible and the possible is sometimes simply a matter of geography.'

The breadfruit tree was fifty paces from the well; with its graduated limbs, it looked like a stairway to the sky. The branches were prodigious: the gnarled limbs more solid than the earth itself. They offered easy footholds and the tree hardly moved as I hauled myself up. I clambered one more level and edged towards a little gap of clear air. It seemed perfect. I took one last look and was horrified to see the glint of a steel blade hacking through the saplings on the other side of the stretch of open scrubland.

A small figure in khaki emerged wielding the machete. I could see a gun slung over one shoulder, The figure moved slowly, testing each step, each breath of air. The monkey huddled up to me. I didn't know what I should do. I only had the little butterfly knife with me, more a talisman than a weapon.

The figure stopped, unstrapped a knapsack and perched on a boulder. The gun was placed next to the knapsack. With the cap also off, it looked like a woman. Her hair fell to her shoulders. She consulted a small device from her knapsack, tapping at it. I was desperate to shield the house, the garden, my fruit trees and crops. If I had my rifle, I thought, would this be the time to use it? To stalk, get close, and then shoot to kill? Wasn't self-protection my right.

She drank from a water canteen, her head flung back. Then she donned her equipment and retreated back into the jungle.

I released my breath. She had turned away from the house, and towards the dried-out river in the south. I reckoned there was enough time to collect the rifle and still catch up with her at the river bend. I dropped to the ground and ran; the little monkey gripping my back. Slipping into the house, I grabbed the rifle and took a short cut past the anthills, checking all the time for signs of any other intruders.

When I reached the river bed the woman was already at the door of a small Explorer Gadfly – a single-seat mini-helicopter – parked in the sand. She packed the back of it with her equipment and then, loosening her uniform, squatted down. I stretched out on the ground, my heart pounding the warm earth. My father, I knew, was an expert marksman. I clipped the telescopic sights into place and lifted the rifle to my shoulder. The stock against my cheek and the steel trigger beneath my finger both felt wet and slippery. My beard prickled. She was now unarmed, motionless; well within range. The cross-hairs on the magnified lens divided her slim figure into four segments. With one bullet her body could be punctured. It would collapse, dehydrate and wilt in the baking sun. Feed our hungry land. Do it now, Jaz implored. If I do this now, will I be safe? Will I save this place? I asked myself. Yes, Kris hissed. If you kill her now, whoever she is, you will at least have some reprieve, and her flying machine to escape in if they ever come looking for her. The little monkey beside me covered its eyes with its small maggoty hands. But I didn't squeeze the trigger. The woman rose, fixed her clothes and climbed into the Gadfly. A moment later it took off with a quick whirr. I remembered how Eldon, my father's father, said he had never even killed an ant. Then, and only then, did I think of Uva.

That evening I persuaded myself that the woman I had seen was only a scout who had temporarily lost her bearings. The geographic, even the military, interest in abandoned coconut plantations for any of the island's warlords must surely be very limited. She must have just stopped to relieve herself on a long cross-country flight. I was sure she had seen nothing worth coming back for, but even so her appearance troubled me. Although I convinced myself there would be no more scouts, I knew I should be more cautious about the signs and markings I made for Uva, the careful cultivation and my programme of renovation. Any stray flight overhead, a re-routed satellite, would notice the vegetable plot, the orchard, the garden and the repaired roof of the house.

In the end I pinned my hopes on the possibility that such an isolated and primitive homestead as mine would be ignored if ever seen from the air. Nevertheless I knew I needed a balance between order and ruin to give me peace on all fronts. The beguiling windmill, my dreams of toil-free irrigation, had to be abandoned. The labour of the bucket soothed my nerves, tired me out so that I could sleep a little more soundly at night. The case of old arrack I had found helped, but it also made me jittery. The screech of the parakeets at sundown, the cries of new jungle birds discovering the orchard sometimes rattled me. The evenings turned fraught. I couldn't stop myself from recalling the figure of the intruder: adjusting her height, her hair, her movement. Comparing it to what I could visualise of Uva. The worst was when I imagined she might have been the one in my sights and that I had not recognised her. I wondered then whether she would have recognised me? A gunman with sunburnt skin and hair in dreadlocks? Perhaps the days had been too many.

Every evening I'd tot up the score on my wooden calendar, again and again, as though they were the beads of a liturgy.

Then one night, having lost count several times, I tripped over my solar lamp. It burst into a thousand sharp stars in the empty pool.

VI

CHRYSALIS

I WOKE up to find the garden full of butterflies. An invasion of small, lace-winged yellow insects hovered over the pool, tumbled off the blossom, sucked and crinkled; they settled on the veranda, the patio, the railings. They seemed to be everywhere, touching, lapping, moistening every surface.

I watched them stretch out over the fence, and on through the lines of coconut trees in a stream of shimmering yellow petals. Feeding, flying, feeding. I went downstairs and waded into the garden. I could feel their wings against my bare skin, brushing soft glitter on my arms and chest. The air was thick with the powder. I was enthralled. I wanted to find their fountainhead. With my sarong hitched up above my knees, I headed for the gate. A few, like saffron droplets, clung on.

Beyond the trees they began to thin out. Their source appeared to be the lake. When I reached the water's edge only a sprinkling of yellow dots remained, steaming in small pools of sunlight. The ground was honeycombed with discarded pupal shells and the lake glistened in the silence. I watched one of the last of the newborn unstretch, hardening a pair of wings for its first flight.

Then the surface of the water broke in a sudden spray of

stripped silver: her closely cropped head, then her gleaming naked body shot up in a terrific breathtaking breach. The whole lake convulsed as it released her ripples.

She pulled me to her, pressing the knot of my sarong against her breasts. I cradled her head, my fingers finding a hard crust of blood behind her ear; ridges and indentations at the rim of her injured skull. I held her close and slipped down to be closer still. In our embrace her skin seemed to become my own. The water of the lake swirled both inside and outside ourselves. She pulled me further into the water, wrapping her legs and arms around me, cupping water with her hand, pouring, sipping. Her breath warm, her lips warm.

I wanted to sing from my heart out, but didn't dare break the moment with a sound.

Her face, streaming, lightened; her eyes flickered, searching behind me, before settling on mine. Her pupils dilated and her flesh untightened. I pulled back and looked again at her face. Her skin was limp beneath the veil of water. There were scratches and grazes on her cheeks and her forehead. I wiped the blood brought to the surface. I ran my fingers around her throat, hoping that what was before me was true and yet not true, her body renewable and herself everlasting. I held her face, waiting for its smile, her words to replace our lost time. 'Did you send them to me? The butterflies?'

She stared at me as though she was stripping back the days, the weeks, the months since we first saw each other by that other stretch of cool green water.

Her fingers moved across mine. 'I need your tongue.' Her voice was hoarse, barely audible. She put her warm wet mouth around mine, pulling back my skin and drawing the sky down around us.

I had been waiting for her for so long that I no longer knew what to say. It was like before, but where were the birds? Her cage? We climbed on to the rock where she had laid out her clothes to dry. She straightened the sleeves of a flat khaki tunic. There were holes among the dark splotches in the front.

'Uniform?'

Uva stared at the water dribbling down from the ends of my hair. When she spoke, her voice was like a disengaged motor. 'I had no choice. Sometimes you have to act as if life in itself is of no value, unless it be your own. To be controlled is to be debased.' Then she lowered her eyes.

I remembered the scout, the uniforms in Farindola. The bursting charge in Kris's grenade that would have blown a hole as big as the pool in my garden when it exploded. I took her hand, tentatively, and we walked back between the coconut trees, following the trail of pulsing yellow confetti to the home I said I had made for us. I kept looking at her as we walked; she kept looking all around her like a cat, watchful, carefully stepping between the congregations of butterflies resting their unyoked wings. When we reached the house, I brought out a chair for her; lit the fire, offered her pounded yam and wild aubergines. I wanted to show her every aspect of the house: the refurbished interior, the nursery with its toy cupboard, my haven upstairs, the flowers in my garden, the birds that flock to the fruit trees, the well of clear water, but her eyes were practically closed. 'I must sleep.' She swallowed a black wad in her mouth; she was exhausted.

★   ★   ★

Her naked body, stretched out before me, looked as though it had been mauled. There were bruises all down her side, her thighs, her breasts, and sores cast like nets on both her shoulders. Every time she breathed the wounds swelled with her expanding skin, oozing a yellowish pus. I adjusted her arms and legs and tried to apply a balm to each of them. Her face hardly flinched.

I sat by her then as I do now, cross-legged, and watched for hours as dream after dream broke under the thin lids of her eyes. I was prepared to wait.

If we had lived in another place, another time, would it have been different? Our sense of life? Would we have been happier walking a towpath beside the Thames? In a garden by Kew? Would we have been safer with rosemary and thyme? Rosebuds? Swallows from Africa? Or are we, like the birds, what we are, no matter where we happen to be?

I know her face will age, as mine; her skin freckle and warp, our love shored and shriven between each fold. Her mouth will wrinkle, her lips crease, I know, even her fingertips. Her eyes will cloud one day, as mine, and conceal what to each other we had revealed – but I thought we had a chance to be ourselves until that true and lasting peace.

I wanted to speak to her, even as she slept, to soothe her; to bring her into the world I had retrieved and to disarm the demons of her past. 'This will be our refuge,' I whispered and kissed the blisters on her lips. I wanted the words to enter her and assuage the pain of her slow recuperation, replenish her memory with my own. Sleep can heal; must. She always said she had its need, a dreamer's need.

Her own words had been few but then a stream of them bubbled close to her lips. She slept the rest of the day and the whole of the night, twitching from time to time. I listened, but could not make out the meaning. I held her hand.

Later I slipped away and placed Kris's knife in a drawer. Now that she was here, with her own, I did not want it to intrude. We each must have our own home, I thought.

I remembered Eldon poking at the rich brown earth under the tall tropical trees of his favourite Palm House. 'This is English soil, isn't it? So how do the roots survive? At some point they must reach that winter outside, don't you think? And get cold?'

'They adapt,' I said with the curt clarity of early adolescence. 'Everything learns to take what it needs.'

'Like babies.' Eldon seemed lost in his thoughts, then he quickly continued. 'I like babies. It is good, you know, to see a baby grow, a son turn into a man. I used to bring your father here when he was growing up. I used to tell him that because of him, I have a place here. A place to belong.'

'I thought you were the one who was meant to give him that.' I was genuinely puzzled.

'I gave him Latin.'

I shrugged. 'Oh, yeah. So?'

'Horace. *They change their climate not their disposition, those who rush across the sea.* They don't teach such things any more, I suppose.'

'Languages?'

'But you see, I didn't understand he was already in too much of a hurry. He's not like you. Lee sees something, he goes for it. He needs to learn patience.' Then he noticed an orange hibiscus bush. 'You know, I think my shoe-flowers are much better than these. They grow outside. To some they might seem flowers of idleness – you know who said that?' He paused. 'Never mind. To me they prove you can change the world.' He touched a petal. 'The place where you think you belong sometimes belongs to you, sometimes it doesn't. But in the end it is the individuals you love that matter, not the place you happen to meet them.'

'I thought you were dead,' Uva moaned the next morning. She screwed her eyes shut against the light. 'I heard shots. Saw you fall. Nothing I could think to do then, but run.'

When she opened her eyes again she looked confused. I didn't know what to think. Our one road seemed irrevocably divided. Her life before we met at her duckweed pond had seemed unreachable; now it seemed most of her life afterwards might be too. But at least she was alive, and so was I.

Out on the veranda I laid out fruit and water for her. I cut open a papaw and removed the black spawn. I squeezed a slice of freckled lime to make small transparent beads over the bright, curved flesh, inanely elated despite the story I had to relate. I thought maybe this time, with my words, we could reclaim what we had lost. I told her how after the soldier got me with his dart, I was taken to a hospital, then a solitary compound. 'I didn't know what had happened to you. I looked for you wherever I could. I even got into the underground mall.'

Uva touched the squashed segment of lime with a finger, and tasted it. 'I know. I was hiding in a village. I heard about the riot. The whisper was of three rebels on the run. From the rumours I knew one had to be you. I knew you would head down here. Jaz I also recognised, difficult though it was to believe he'd do anything so daring off a catwalk.' She paused, surprised by her own torrent. Her sharp brows knitted together as though she was drawing two worlds into one, her tongue was stuck between her teeth. Then she shivered and the rest of her words sputtered out. 'I tried to follow you, but it was impossible. No one could move. Our network came apart. Everyone who could help was gone. All disappeared. Not a soul was left to trust . . . Even Zeng was gone. Disappeared.'

'Zeng? You went back to Maravil?'

'No, to his commune, but he'd been taken. They were executing anyone they had the slightest suspicion about.' She let the breath she'd held in rush out; her eyes folded once more. 'A nightmare.'

I remembered the exhilaration escaping with Jaz while Maravil burned; I hadn't worried about anybody else at the time. Certainly not Zeng. 'I went to him. I thought he could help me find out if you were caught or already on your way here. He was the one who got me underground. They must have found out.' I wanted her to reassure me that somehow all that had happened was worthwhile, that all her comrades knew the risks they were taking, and that the grip of the military had been weakened by its own desire for vengeance.

Uva did not respond; she stared at her hands, deaf to me. 'The only way I could see to get through to the jungle and round the hill country was to become a soldier myself.' She paused again. Her fingers clenched tight. I put my hand over her fist. It quivered under my fingers as if about to explode. She was shivering some more. 'Do you understand?'

'A soldier?'

With a frown, she slowed down her breathing until the shaking stopped. The skin around her eyes was still weary; puffy. Her breath became shallow. 'I took the clothes, the identity of one of them. He was an officer. I picked him up in a slut bar by the minefields. He was due to take charge of a new batch of youngsters. They were going to train in the jungle for a new offensive. Perfect for me.' She turned and gazed out across the treetops; she would not look at me any more. Her eyes were glassy. Her voice rose. 'I killed him. I frigged him out of his uniform and while he was wiping his prick I killed him.' Her fist jerked free and jabbed upward towards my chest, swift and sure. 'I stabbed him four times in the heart.'

I grabbed her hand, this time with both of mine, and forced it back down on to the table. 'It's over now. You are here. Put it out of your mind. You have to forget it.' At that moment I didn't care what she had done to reach me.

She wrested her hand away, toppling her spoon from the table. 'Forget? How can you say that? You of all people.'

'I'm sorry,' I mumbled. The spoon lay like a metal eye coated with sand where she had wet it with her saliva. I stared at it. Everything was sliding out of reach. Who was she now? Who was I? Why did it feel like the world was a trap? Have I, like my father, and perhaps even my grandfather, wanted too much? Wanted too much in coming here? Wanted too much in Uva? Wanted too much to make the brief life we had last for ever? Wanted too much to find her, and myself, after wanting so little for so long? 'Look, I'll get you another spoon.' I stood up determined to keep steady and left her, quickly, in a silence that was as painful as it was invasive. How could I tell her to forget when all I ever wanted in my life was to remember, and to be remembered? How could I? Now I wanted only to help her, and for her to help me. I knew she needed to tell me all the things I didn't want to hear; she needed me like she had never needed me before. When I saw that, it made me feel even more alive than I had felt with her by the sea; as if somehow our real journey that had been interrupted at the beach hotel could finally begin again at a higher pitch despite her seeming to be, at that moment, further away than she had ever been from me.

Sunlight streamed through the sweeping fronds and but-terfly bushes: warm, tempered, life-giving. Shadows ripened across the sand. The garden was blooming. A sparrow flitted between two spidery shrubs. We had been given the chance to renew our lives. I wanted to tell her that here she could be released from all the wrongs of the past; I just didn't know how to. Not yet. To live, perhaps we have to learn to lie.

By the time I returned, she had left the table. She was at the well, washing her face. She finished and, wrapping a towel around her bare body, strolled over to the edge of the garden. There she collected some dry brown leaves, a few broken twigs, and piled them up in a small pyre. When I went over, she asked me to light it.

'Why?'

She waited until the flames caught before replying. 'I want to burn this. Burn it like everything else that has come between us.' She threw her uniform on to the fire. 'Two tucks and that uniform did everything for me. Everything. I became a real leader. I took command of his squad of new recruits. They didn't know what to expect, but I knew that with them I could get out. They were young. Just boys in awe of big stripes, the cat's eye. Orphans from a village. Children without hope. I planned an expedition to take us right across the mountains. I thought that they too might find a new life, if we could get free.' She watched the smoke drift up into the coconut.

'They brought you here? Children?' I watched her lower lip draw in; thin frets gather around her mouth.

'I told them this was no game; I told them we were surrounded by enemies. I could speak their language. I told them we have to move like shadows. Take out bridges, trax, watchtowers if we have to. Commandos are what we are, I said. Very special commandos. The boys asked no questions.

They were quick to learn. We did two hits and then broke out of the cordon. Crossed the river to the south. They love strong leadership. Clarity. They were good, devoted boys: Pambu, the youngest, was our baby, then there was Muwan, the most beautiful boy, and Kadu, second-in-command, strong and caring. Each one was a hero.' She spoke with both pride and sorrow in her voice. I thought of Ismail and the youngsters in the jungle. If only we could live in a world that valued its children, and protected their childhood.

'Where are they? What's happened to your boys?' I asked.

'I forgot the air. My big, big mistake. We were attacked from the air. I didn't even know who they were. Everywhere fireballs whooshed. The ground disappeared. I was scouting ahead. Leading us out of danger, I thought. Out of danger . . . I just didn't imagine it would come from the air: strafing, bombing, burning. Annihilation.'

'None of them survived?'

'I raced back to them. I was screaming. I tried to drag Kadu out of the flames but his arms had been ripped off by a blast. And then Muwan . . .' Uva squeezed her eyes shut. 'His head exploded right in front of me. Pieces of him went everywhere.' She tugged at her non-existent hair.

'Pambu's stomach was sliced open. He was trying to hold it together but the stuff was spilling out of his hands. When he looked up I saw he had only half his face left. He had no mouth. My baby. I shot him, looking at him. He could see me with his one eye. Do you know what I'm saying? I had to pump the bullets into his brain to stop his pain . . . I can't bear it.' She jammed a hand to her mouth and turned to walk back up to the house alone.

★   ★   ★

I waited for the remnants of her gruesome journey to turn to ash. The uniform burnt slowly; the white smoke billowed up obscuring the blossom I had trailed across a small archway separating the orange from the lilac. I realised then that between the moment I fell, shot by a soldier, and her reappearance from the waters of the lake, having been a soldier, too many deaths had blotched our separate lives to allow for a simple return to our beginnings. I poked the embers with a stick, turning them over. Another piece of cloth caught fire and for a moment I could see, in the flame, the figure of the man whose place she had taken, and the flickering outlines of the other men whose lives she had had to take. I shut my eyes trying to fill my head with the wild lime, the coconut, the exuberance of the flowers of my cherished garden. Now that she was here, I told myself, nothing else must matter.

When the fire burnt itself out, I raked over the cinders. Although few hardy branches remained, all of the cloth had gone.

Using a picker I had made, I lopped a young coconut and took it back up to the house. Uva was sitting by the empty pool, legs drawn up, clasping her feet. I gave her coconut water to drink. She cradled the husk with both hands and drank out of the hole I had punched until a small stream leaked out of the side of her mouth. I tried to stem it with mine, but she jerked her head back.

'The uniform is all burnt,' I said to mollify her and, perhaps, protect myself.

She studied me as though she was looking at something so long lost that she could no longer remember what it was.

'What's happened, has happened. We can't change it. But

now we have a future together.' I tried to kiss her again. 'We are the only ones here.'

She pushed me away, muttering under her breath.

She wouldn't speak again all day but that night, in bed, her hands moved over me, under me. Her fingers were thin and bony; her nails sharp, uneven and torn.

She placed her hard lips over mine, her vulva on my knee. Her tongue in my mouth was bitter, as though tears had dripped inside her. The cracks in her skin had not yet healed but all of a sudden she regained her strength: her fingers dug into me. She pulled my whole body around hers even as she enfolded mine.

In the morning the flowers all around the garden looked jostled. A big black bumble-bee droned out of one and wobbled, heavily, into another. High up above us a lapwing called. In all the time I had been alone, I had never heard the lapwing's tease. I thought thankfully things must have changed.

'Did you hear it?' I asked her, but she didn't even smile. She could find nothing amusing in the birdcall, or in anything else in our lives any more.

A small greenish bird with a curved honey bill whirred, hanging in the air; a blue-tailed bee-eater swooped out of the yellow-blossom tree.

She came up to me, later in the day, while I was watering the flowers. Her knife was in a necklace hanging between her breasts.

'You haven't told me what happened to my Jaz? And who the other man was? Where did they go?'

I emptied the bucket into a bed of cannas and placed it upside-down on the ground. I took her hand; she let me stroke each finger, one at a time. I imagined her fist around other flesh, younger, and felt a yearning for a wholeness to be where there was only a hollow. With emptiness, I now know, we lose balance. My early suspicions about Kris and Uva resurfaced. I didn't want to bring him to where we were. I didn't want to revive him, or any pain. I wished that his knife had been destroyed along with everything else up in Farindola so that nothing remained of the past. But for her sake I had to explain something of what had happened. Slowly I reconstructed the bare facts of our journey, avoiding Kris's actual name. I told her how Jaz kept us going, joking, talking, feeding, and how he held back the soldiers in Farindola, shooting until he was shot. Suppressing the brutality of Jaz's body's being ripped apart, blotting out those images, I repeated instead Jaz's last words about her, reclaiming a world of love, reshaping as he would our momentary lives.

'Farindola. That was where my parents wanted to remake the world,' Uva said quietly, as though this piece of history might provide some comfort. 'My mother said that at the top of the world we could begin again, a world more worthwhile, a way of life that would flow down across the whole island, right down to the coast, like a great river of alluvial water.'

'You know it then.' I tried to see her other life behind her eyes. 'There was something about that place. I wondered whether you might have been there. We could have stayed in Farindola, except we started out all wrong . . .'

'How did you find it?' Curiosity seemed to overcome any sign of grief for Jaz.

I was glad and yet uncomfortable that she found it so easy. 'We were following the only road we could. Our guide thought it would lead us down here . . .'

'But who was it? You haven't told me.'

The muscles in my stomach tightened. What could I say without dragging all of what had gone before into the free space I wanted to preserve for us? But then I thought, what could it matter now? He was gone. All of that was over. Our life was nothing, surely, if it could be overshadowed by a ghost. 'You knew him too,' I sighed. 'Kris, the metalworker.'

'Kris?' Her face turned hard, disbelieving.

Does it matter? Does it matter? The old mantra jingled in my ear.

'Kris took you to Farindola?' She spoke as if to herself.

'It seemed the only way to go; he didn't know the road stopped at the top.'

'He knew it all right.'

I tried to swallow my disbelief. 'Was he expecting you there?'

'He'd rather see me dead than in Farindola.'

She was wrong. 'No, he wanted to help . . .'

'Kris has never helped anyone but himself in his whole life.'

'But he helped us all along.'

'You he needed, until he needed you no more. He was in a hole in Maravil. He just used you to escape. I know him.' Uva gripped my hand and hissed. 'Believe me, I do.'

If it was ever love, I wondered, how could it turn to such loathing? I pictured the knife he had carried in devotion. 'Come, I have something to show you.' I led her quickly up to the house. From the dresser drawer I pulled out his knife. 'Look.' I thrust it at her. 'This matches yours, doesn't it? He made it because he loved you.'

She grabbed the knife. 'No, he didn't. My father made this. And he made mine. How did you get it?'

'It was in the plane he was fixing.'

'Plane?'

I told her about the aircraft.

'His escape . . .'

'I don't think so. The knife was wrapped up like a gift. It was a gift. I am sure of it. He knew how much I wanted it. I knew it was a sort of twin . . .'

'Was he not the one who was going to fly your peacock plane? Was he not the one who brought those soldiers to you?' Uva peered into my eyes, grasping me with both her hands. 'Can't you see what he was up to?'

'I don't know.' I released myself from her grip.

'He was my brother. He betrayed my father. He fancied he'd be the hero and get to run all my father's projects – make Farindola his own. The bastards used him to get my father and then they dumped him.'

'Your brother?' His strained movements immediately began to fit a pattern I had never before imagined. His sharp looks, his constant tenseness, the inner drive. Even so I couldn't work him out. If only I had known he was her brother. 'He never said anything.' I retrieved the knife and weighed it in my hand. It was as light as a prayer. 'I don't know what he was thinking of doing, but he was on our side, I am sure of it. I think he wanted to stay in Farindola. He was fixing the plane for Jaz and me. For us to leave him there. Maybe to make his amends alone. He had changed from the person you knew, I am sure of it. He blew himself up to let me escape.'

For the rest of the day we moved in awkward uncertain circles, intersecting only when I went to fill another bucket and had to cross the trench she was digging between the crop garden and the well. She dug with fanatical determination, heaping the soil around her in a succession of small pyramids.

I wanted to ask her more about Kris and their parents. Why had she never mentioned a brother before? Why had he betrayed their father? How? What was their father really like, for Kris to turn so against him? But I resisted for fear of upsetting her. 'What is it? What are you digging?' I asked instead.

She wouldn't answer; she continued attacking the earth single-mindedly, the way Kris would sometimes continue with something he was intent on, with no sign of communication. I began to see similarities in the way she moved, the way she gripped a handle. I couldn't understand how could they grow in such apparently different directions.

She wouldn't stop digging until the trench was as big as her. Then she climbed out and went to the remains of the fire where the previous day she had burnt her uniform. She undid her sarong and scooped up all the ashes in it; she carried it, like an offering, to the trench. She laid it lengthways and folded one half over the ash and cinders. Then she buried it all, shovelling back the earth she had dug up, stamping on it with her bare feet.

When she finally finished she crouched down, ready to pounce on anything that might move, her whole naked body wet with her labour.

The sun was setting over the orchard. I didn't know how to reach her. 'Come to the well,' I entreated. 'Let me bathe you.' I wanted a hundred pails of water to wash away those tears, her wounds. I wanted her to heal soon, and myself too, and drop all the scabs of her ugly past.

★   ★   ★

That third night she lay sleepless next to me staring out at the sky, her body tired and yet tense as it must have been for months. I ran my fingers along a weal on her shoulder. She made no response. 'Are you thinking of Kris?' I asked. She rolled the other way; back taut, hot, choking in pain, or rage. I waited, breathing as close to her as possible until each of our exhalations seemed to be in unison. When her breath was finally steady again, she muttered, 'I can't sleep. I know I must, but I can't. Every time I close my eyes I see . . .' Her voice receded.

I tried to hold on to it. 'You see what?'

Her breath stopped.

'Tell me. What do you see?'

'Them. In pieces all over. Lumps burning.'

I saw the bodies of Jaz and Kris before the grenade detonated; but Uva, I guess, saw many, many more. Her dismembered children exploding, spewing blood; her mother, her father.

I waited for her breathing to slow down again before speaking. 'It is not your fault.'

'But it is. I should have known better. I should have done something. I let it happen to my parents. Then I let it happen to them, my children.'

'You can't blame yourself for everything. You did what you could. You are lucky to have survived. There is no wrong in it. We are here now. At least we have each other.' I held her tighter. What more could I say? It would be her words that would heal her, I knew, not mine.

Outside, the leaves of the coconut, the jak, the breadfruit tree shifted in the breeze, unmasking the stars whose light began to pierce the gloom of the night even as they died in their own place. Blood flooded the inside of my head like a tide released by the moon to revive the beach that was nearly our own. There was pain in each of our breaths; but with every pulse that pushed my blood another fraction further through the cycle of this earth, I felt able to believe a little more that our lives somehow will be replenished.

I saw my mother. She had sunglasses wrapped around her eyes. We were staying in a hotel with pink walls and pine trees in the garden and steps leading down to hot white sand. I remember her mostly from a photograph of that summer. Sitting on a wall, searching the sea through her thick black sunglasses, twisting the loops of a gold thread in her fingers. A wordless figure who made me always feel I was a trespasser in her life. The Mediterranean, I was told, was what she was looking at; she preferred it to any other sea. I remembered Grandma Cleo coaxing her, 'Penny, my dear, you must give him time. All we can ever give each other in this life is time.'

In the morning, down by the well, I found the monkey scrabbling around Uva's refilled trench. It had pawed away some of the earth and rolled a coconut into a dip at one end, like a skull. When it saw me, it started hooting as if to call up the dead. I was furious. I shouted at it and kicked the coconut out. The monkey hobbled away, chattering.

Uva heard us and came to the railing upstairs. She called out to me, worried. 'What's the matter? Don't scold the poor thing. What's it done?'

I didn't answer; I was relieved to see that familiar concern on her face again.

With each passing day she seemed to go a little further into the garden. She'd spend days examining the stems, the leaves, the flowers I had tended. She'd say very little, but I'd listen to every word. I asked her more about what will happen than what had happened. Simple questions about the life of plants: which of them will flower tomorrow, and which next week? Which will produce fruit? And when? I thought it was better to get her to look ahead. It seemed to work. She had no difficulty identifying ones which I had found no trace of in my gardener's annuals. Slowly, as she followed me, she began to pull out weeds, train the beans and the marrow. Sometimes she'd step in and space out the plants that seem destined to become entangled with each other, and succour those that needed more nursing. Soon she was drawing patterns for crossbreeding like some gene-genie on the loose.

By the afternoon though, when the sky turned lazurite, she'd flag; the whole garden would subside. Then, as now, I would sit by her, listening for her breath. The earth itself was in need of repose. In the stillness, the quiet, the sense of being reprieved seemed, for the moment, to alleviate all the suffering of the world. I knew this could not be true, but I needed to believe it might be.

When the sun dropped, and the day became a little cooler, we'd sometimes walk together up to the lake where we had been reunited. I showed her where I first came ashore, where I took apart the aircraft. I showed her my early trails, the signs I had made for her and she pointed out the one that had alerted her. Beneath the tree on which I had carved my first initial, she found a hefty green melon.

'Is it edible?' I had to ask.

She split it open with her knife. 'What you have to do is suck it and see,' she explained patiently.

She flicked a few black seeds out of the wedge before lifting it to her mouth and sucking it, hard. The red flesh turned white. 'If it is bitter you spit the poison out; if it is nectar you take it all.'

As her skin healed, a residue of that sparkle I had first seen in her by the pond near the Palm Beach Hotel slowly returned to her eyes. When she walked past the empty pool, I wished it were full again, as it must have been once, to reflect her on its undulating surface and fill every element with her moving shape. The emerald pigeons, the flying fish, the baskets of fruit all seemed close once more.

'What do you think about this pool?' I asked her one evening. She was stretched out on a planter's chair, under the pergola teeming with ever more white trumpets in the failing light; her breasts flat underneath the thin muslin of an old shawl. She had started to listen more, as though at last the explosions in her ears had died away. 'I wanted to clean it – all that dried algae – and fill it. I had a grand plan: an Archimedean screw, a windmill, a cistern with aqueducts. A tremendous plan, but then I was afraid it might attract too much attention if it was spotted from the air.'

She smiled for the first time since she arrived. 'A pool would not make such a difference. They say there are old ponds and pools dotted all over from here to the coast. But Archimedean? Why so complicated?'

'I didn't think I could fill it just using a pail.'

'What about the pipe? They must have had some system. They didn't have slaves here, did they?'

'The pipes are there.' I pointed to the grilles on each wall. 'But there is no tap.'

She shook her head, bemused. 'I don't know how you've

survived on your own for so long.' She stood up and inspected the stonework around the pool. Then she went straight to a slab at one corner. It was loose. She moved it; underneath was the wheel of a valve. 'Look, here it is. The inlet from the lake. They must have a pipe up there to divert the waters into the pool. Then, when you want, you open one on the other side to let it drain out. Into the garden. It goes out and lifts up the water table. That is why you have those big trees over there. Those are thirsty trees. You can see how they were growing years ago when this house was once before like your little pleasure dome.' She opened the valve but nothing flowed. 'We have to find the stopcock up at the lake.'

'Where? How can you trace the pipe? There is no sign on the ground to show where it goes. I can't see anything. You'd have to be a water diviner.'

Uva stepped back with her hands on her hips, exasperated, but looking much more like her old self. 'Diviner? No, an engineer. Where would you connect it up?'

She too was a real fixer.

'What?'

'Nothing.'

'Where's your map?'

We went over to my painted board.

She pointed out where she reckoned the pipe would be. 'Let's go.'

It took us less than an hour to locate it. There was another small wheel set in a culvert grown over with maidenhair. She hit the spindle with a stick to loosen it. 'Be careful,' I warned but the valve opened. I heard the water flow.

We filled the pool to the brim so that when we slipped in, the water ran over and darkened the sand with its abundance. Yellow flowers floated between us. When Uva came out of the water they stuck to her like the butterflies who had appeared before on their brief, dazzling pilgrimage home.

That evening we ate pumpkin, cowpea and cassava. For fruit she had picked mangosteen and a durian.

'Have you tried?' She asked me with a hint of the mischief she used to display at the beach.

I was a little apprehensive of the durian's prickly shape and its odour. She scoffed at my reluctance. 'It is so rare to find these still growing. Even in the old days a really fresh durian was the most sought-after aphrodisiac.'

'Really?' I was not convinced.

'Here, try the mangosteen first then.' She smiled again, breaking the purple shell in her hand to reveal snowdrops from heaven.

Later we watched the moon bob in the pool, licked by the flames of the candles I had floated for her.

'Will we live here for ever?' Her voice slipped over me, her lips warm and thick like an engorged flower.

I held her in my hands and pressed her. 'Yes.'

'And when there are no more matches for the fire?'

'We'll have to keep burning all the time.' I wished, too late, I had not said it.

She rescued a mynah with a damaged wing, and a mongoose trapped in the cowshed. She nursed them until the monkey, the mynah and the young mongoose all ate right out of her hand. She even drew the bees from their hives. 'I wish I had some milk,' she said and blinked at the look that passed over my face. 'No, not from me – I was spiked.'

I didn't know what she meant, but I could sense the walls around her early traumas crumbling. She tried to purse her lips, but the words gushed out.

'During the Emergency, anyone whom the authorities deemed rebellious was sterilised. Spiked. Spayed. It happened at school. First a dart, like yours, you know? Then a scraper. That was when my parents decided we had to escape up into the hills. To Farindola. But Kris wouldn't come. He was mad. He was mad at my father. Kris didn't agree with anything he said or did. Our school system had warped him much sooner than my parents expected; before they realised it. You see, he thought my father wanted to control him. He didn't understand my father was only trying to encourage some spirit, grow back the wildness in us, no? My parents believed that diversity gave us strength; that love grew stronger when it had to hold things together: unity in diversity. It's true. But Kris saw everything differently. For months my parents tried to persuade him to leave the city and come and join us in Farindola. But every time he came he would quarrel and storm off. He didn't see the corruption. He didn't believe that the bush squads who broke the bones of their victims one by one, beat them and burnt them with firebrands, pulped the organs of infants, were officials doing their duty. He saw *us* as the destroyers. He went and informed. They came then with an executioner and took over Farindola for themselves.' She hunched her shoulders, shrinking. 'All I could do then was to go from town to town like a little hothouse breeder – the last of our line – carrying plants, small animals. Wild viruses to infect their whole regime.' She hammered her knees with her fists and straightened up as though she had to inspire another army.

I was crestfallen. Here, in this garden, I had imagined we might become the beginning of something new. The core of a story told and retold, imagined as I had so often imagined my own parents meeting, or my grandparents – Eldon and

Cleo – discovering, in their inexplicable wartime courtship along the Strand, that yellow birds and dragonflies were not unique to the air currents of their separate island homes. The stuff of legends, like even Uva's own transformation from farmer to warrior to farmer again. I recalled Pushpa, the little girl in the camp, and wished she could have been reborn to us here and have at least a glimpse of a world free from strife.

The animal in Uva's arms whined; she stroked it, calming the mongoose, and herself, down. 'This little pup needs some real nourishment.'

She nurtured it with water, wild herbs and crushed fruit until the mongoose and the monkey learnt to play with each other in the sand, around the pool, and among the coconut trees as children might in a garden of trust.

As more flowers and fruit trees blossomed, more birds appeared. Each day a new flash of colour, a different melody in the garden. Uva would sit up in bed with a cotton sheet wrapped around her and listen in wonder. The patterns in the air became increasingly vivid and complex. As one song ascended, another descended; elaborating first light, day by day.

'Where do they come from?' she asked.

'I don't know,' I said. 'I couldn't believe it, at first. There are salaleenas, parakeets, wagtails and bee-eaters.'

'Wagtails?'

'Sure. Why not?'

She laughed then, bursting a warm pod within her; a sound I had not heard for longer than I could remember, a sound from the edge of heaven. I felt that we were, at last, where we belonged. Among trees mute yet more perfect than us; their roots nourished by the whole of the earth's past, and harbouring the future already in their buds. And that in time there might even be children from the forest who would come to us and grant our lives too a sense of perpetuity.

The next day Uva showed me how to extract dyes from vegetables; to turn straw into cloth like a weaverbird; to make soap out of coconut and oil for cooking, for massaging the inner and the outer flesh, for lighting the lamps at nights and lubricating all the spinning chakras in a body. She tapped a rubber tree, slashing it with her knife, and collected the sticky milk in a coconut shell. Dipping her fingers in raw latex she painted the bearded aurora around my nipples, and laughed again when the tree above squeaked, rocked by the wind that blew from the ocean churning far away.

One night she pressed her head back against me and opened my palm. 'My mother should have seen you.'

'Like this?'

'Your hand.' She traced my knotted heartline with her fingernail and ran her teeth along the edge of my palm.

I pulled my hand away. 'Why?'

'Her grandmother had always told her about a man with a hand like this. See these three crosses. Someone who will change the world they lived in for ever.'

'Did it ever happen?'

She turned her head and looked up drowsily, before closing her eyes. 'I never could stay awake long enough to hear the end of her stories.'

In the dark I mulled over her words. I thought about my own mother and father: their insomnia in a world spinning noisily out of control. The throb of traffic, aeroplanes, babies; the threat of cyclones from nowhere. What did they wish for? A change for the better? Did they too live their lives with a growing sense of unease about the world they would bequeath? But how did he ever think that a fighter plane's brash pre-emptive strike, blowing up somebody else's home, could improve it? And she that her death would? Then I recalled Eldon's words about how we each go our own way to seek the light we need, how we each find the balance that becomes survival. We have to. But what did his life amount to: basking pointlessly above the clouds for years and coming down only to grow flowers in a foreign land. I could imagine his reply: *mutato nomine de te fabula narratur . . . Change but the name and the tale is of you.*

I wished I could tell him that I did learn some of that stuff too, when I needed to.

When my father left, he went without saying a word; not a word to me. He mussed my hair, patted the dog, and that was it. All I ever heard was my mother's excuses for his absence, repeated again and again. 'It's his work: aviation advice, training, that sort of thing. An opportunity he could not afford to miss.' A quick smile, a wave out of an open sunroof, and he had gone. But he had told his own mother, Cleo, a slightly different story. 'I have some things to sort out. For him, you know. His past is my future.' For some reason I had always assumed that he had meant me in saying this, but now I know he had meant his father, not his son.

'I think in the end you have to learn to live on your own.' Uva ruminated as if to herself, sitting on the steps of the veranda. She had carved another figurine with her knife and was lifting it up to the light to examine the wings.

'But you are with me now.' I was busy refitting a wheel to an old pushcart.

'I know. But the more I see you, the more I can see how empty life would be without you now.'

'You shouldn't think like that. We should be thankful for what we have been given.' I pushed the retaining pin in; the wheel spun freely.

'My mother wanted to be connected to everything around her, and yet she did everything to be completely self-sufficient.' Uva looked around her as though she was seeing her mother's home again. 'The centre of our house was a processing plant: we made our own flour, our own furniture, our own cloth . . . everything. And now we have to do it here, again.'

I put down the pushcart and went over to her. I took her by the hand. 'But you are not alone. We are never entirely on our own, even here. We rely on people who were here before us. We have to. Look at this house, the chairs, the roof, the bed, the pushcart. We repair, rebuild . . .'

'Like scavengers?' She looked at me doubtfully.

'Sure, why not? Scavenge. Salvage. We must use what we discover. Make it our history.'

'And then?'

'Leave things a little bit better for those who come after us.'

Her face hardened again. 'There'll be nobody after us here.'

'But there will be. Others like us. Others who escape, who break through. Maybe even orphans from the forest. They will need all the help they can get.'

'What for?'

'To build a life. A little time for themselves. If they find this place, they will know it is possible to be free. To love. To find each other.'

She ran a finger down the side of her nose slowly, brooding over the prospect of strangers in our midst. 'I think our time is too short. I don't want anybody else to come even near here, ever. No rebels, no refugees, no orphans, no soldiers, not even a scout. Never.'

For a moment, my heart failed.

'What's the matter?'

I told her about the scout who had come in the Gadfly.

'You let her go back?'

'She was only looking . . .'

'Did she have a gun?'

I nodded. 'But if she didn't go back, others would have come looking for her —'

'She had a gun,' Uva cut in. 'She'd have used it on you, if she had seen you. They are killers. The only way to stop a killer is by killing her, or him, first.' She took my face in her hands, her expression fixed as though each point she was about to make was linked inexorably to the next. 'Sometimes you have to sacrifice your innocence to protect this world that you care so much for, that you believe in. Sometimes we have to risk going too far, otherwise we risk losing everything. You must understand that, after all we've been through.' Her own eyes closed in the shadow of the orchard trees. 'One bullet in the right place might have saved both my father and my mother. There is a link between life and death; Kris's and theirs. We all need to discover who we are and where we stand; find our own special balance between what we know ought to be, and what we can see has to be done.'

Her thin, creased lids trembled behind her welded lashes.

I remembered the mothers with their children; Ismail and his band of urchins with their contorted lives and their sad, unflinching eyes. Were they then driven too late to the gun? Perhaps she was right, but then was Kris right too? What is balance? To protect according to your own need, to avenge as the old gods do? Were they all correct and Eldon wrong? Maybe the bullet does fly both ways when you pull a trigger, maybe each time we do learn a little more about what it is to be alive, just as we see more clearly between each blink of an eye, each lapse.

When the last glow of the sun receded, I lit a candle at her feet. And then another and another like a belt around us both. As night grew I showed her the new fireflies illuminating the bushes, a handful of old stars crackling through the clouds. We were safe, I said. I was sure. One way or another. In bed we slept within each other's milky lips, counting the seconds by each other's heartstops, living and dying one after another, the rifle with its gloaming sights nestled under the net.

'Last night I dreamt we were back in the jungle. Somebody was hunting us.' She reached out and touched my face. She had shadows under her eyes but everywhere else were signs of rapid regeneration. A thin wash of gold seeped into the sky. 'You were younger. There was a roar. I could not hear what you were saying. I saw you slither down a small damp muddy track. I followed you. I saw an arrow in the sky falling. When we reached it, you picked it up. Behind you was the biggest waterfall I have ever seen. The sound of the water was deafening. Across the canyon the river was at our height: a hand gripping a huge black rock, the cascade like its fingers. The water just fell, and fell, unendingly. You were mesmerised. I could feel the spray.'

'Is that what woke you up?'

'Why? Was it you?'

I moistened the tendons of her throat; the skin around her Adam's apple glistened. I wanted only for that moment to last. 'Water is life, isn't it? Your dream must have come to restore you.'

'I remember now. I was hungry. There was a fruit tree but I couldn't reach the fruit.'

'Close your eyes,' I said, and pressed a small, ripe mango to her. 'You can't pluck fruit from a dream tree.' I brushed her roughened nipples with my lips. I kissed her and she kissed me too.

In the garden, I counted the notches I had cut since she had arrived; the next would be our fiftieth.

Early the following morning, I was woken by the insistent song of a bulbul. Uva didn't stir. The bird seemed to come closer and then go away again. I got out of bed without disturbing the deep sleep she had at last been able to reach. I followed the song down into the garden. I wanted to see our latest arrival; perhaps even catch it for her. I looked for the songster among the orange and pink blossom, the light purple hearts of the sprawling bush by the fence, between the crabclaws and the canebursts. I followed its fletched notes all the way down to the crop garden. But all I ever saw was the movement of small leaves, the spring of a twig as the bird left each temporary perch and slipped further out of sight in a ruffled slipstream of warm air.

Then at the edge of the garden I discovered the remains of a freshly eaten mango, much larger than the one I had picked for her the previous day. The seed had been freshly sucked as I might have sucked it, or she, but neither of us had been to this particular tree for days.

The grass was bent in a trail that petered out and I couldn't tell what was there and what I imagined to be there. Near the lower branches of the tree there were bootmarks in the earth where someone had jumped. They were not my bootmarks, and Uva had not worn anything but a toe-ring and rubber sandals on her feet since the day she arrived. In one sharp indent I found the crushed remains of a small spotted copper moth.

The blood hurt as it surged inside my chest. It was not fear I felt but the vulnerability of everything I loved. There was no telling where the intruder might be by now. Perhaps even at the house. The shaggy roof, the still, drowsy coconut trees, the splashes of colour around the garden – Uva's bougainvillaea – and her easily named morning-glory made a peaceful and contented picture. I was sure I'd feel it, if it was already encroached, as she would. So close to the ground we have learnt to live.

I crept back into the house and collected the rifle and a sarong to cover myself.

She was up, uncoupled from the bed. She was taking in the sun on her bare skin to heal the last vestiges of her early wounds.

'The gun?' She looked surprised.

'There's somebody around,' I replied, keeping my voice low.

She slipped down, quickly tying a robe around her. 'Are you sure?'

I told her about the mango seed.

'Could have been the monkey, no? Where is he anyway?'

'I don't know. I haven't seen him this morning. But it wasn't, I'm sure. I saw the bootmarks. Big dents on the ground where he – or she – had jumped up for it.'

'If he's seen the house he'll know it is inhabited. Since he has not come forward, he has either gone for help, or is scouting some more. Either way he has got to be found.'

'I know.' The words seemed more sombre to me than they had ever been before.

Uva went into the kitchen and collected a machete. 'I'll take this and my knife, you take the gun.'

'Are you sure?'

Her face was still. Her head lowered as though with the weight of pain in her hard black eyes. 'Have you ever used a knife to kill someone?'

I looked back at the garden. 'I haven't even used a gun. Not to kill.' I pulled back the bolt; the first bullet was in the breech. I swallowed hard. The cords in my throat were taut. It seemed at that moment I no longer had a choice.

Uva said she would sweep around the northern edge and that I should follow the path past the fruit trees. 'We'll meet where the old river turns. Don't shoot unless you have to. There may be more than one. We have to be sure to get them all.' She moved swiftly, barefoot. I would have preferred for us to have gone together, but she was the one who knew how to fight. I was not frightened of who we might find; I feared only my own desire. My desire for our life to be everlasting.

I stole along the wall looking for a sign indicating the direction the intruder might have taken. I wanted my eyes to be hawks. *Think as they would, your prey.* Uva's way: be one with the ground, with all that is on it. One earth, one mind. Hunt as you love, bound unto death. We do it because we must. For love as we know it. I circled the garden and tried to imagine the path anyone coming upon the enclosure might take.

By the ironwood tree I stopped. If only the bulbul would fly out, up in the air, and give a signal. The sun seemed to burn in a way it had not done for ages. My whole body was drenched in sweat. I could see our lives in the days to come, the months and years I would measure with notches and crosses, with hand-harvests and orange blossom, full of butterflies and moths, parakeets and pigeons. The earth will be green, the sky blue. We will learn to live with small acts of self-protection, merciless deaths and the troubled acceptance of a price that will sometimes seem too high for true survival. Ours will be a need to forget as much as to remember. My father had returned home. I understood that now. In our ruptured world it was not where I had been, but a place I could only imagine. It was the same for me. I did not want to leave here. I would not cross the sea again.

Ahead, the razor-leaf bamboo by the dry river-bed creaked. I slipped the safety catch off the gun. It felt lighter than before. I moved ahead slowly, crouching, my eye trained on the yellow segments swaying in the warm wind, the stiletto leaves. The clump of bamboo was too thick for anyone to be in it, but beyond, in the dry river-bed, a platoon could be waiting and I would not know it. Death could be there and I would not know it. Let there be light and let our lives be free. Let us not lose more than can ever be gained. Skirting the bamboo, I dropped down through a line of wild coffee shrubs. The berries were hard but still impregnated the air with their pungent smell. I wanted her; nothing else ever. Then, there on the steep ground, I stumbled over a dozing soldier. Jolted out of his slumber, he whined at me. I was too startled to do anything. He was close enough for me to see the furrows streaking his forehead, a small fuzzy dimple quivering under his lower lip. His face dissolved into Nirali's outside the Palm Beach Hotel. I couldn't bring the gun to bear. He grovelled before me. Suddenly he struck out and rolled away. Only then did I see the other soldiers in the hollow beyond. Their hands were red with the blood of the monkey they had butchered between them. They had stuck its head on a pole and set fire to its tail. They had come to take everything. The captain saw me and began to shout, raising his arms.

I gripped the gun hard. Forgive, forget, I once might have said, flee if we must – but I squeezed the trigger instead and worked the bolt again and again. Gunfire stuttered in my hands killing the captain first and then two more before I saw a figure fly in the air, jerking, twisting and turning like a ribbon. She leapt on the last man with her butterfly knife opening in one hand and a sun-stained machete in the other, swinging low and unremitting, between the hail of my bullets. She slew him as she fell.

Then the whole sky darkened as a legion of trident bats, disturbed from their brooding trees by the gunshots, took to the newly burnt air, drawing a broken eclipse over another fragile world for ever altered; riven.

A NOTE ON THE TYPE

The text of this book is set in Bembo. The original types for which were cut by Fracesco Griffo for the Venetian printer Aldus Manutius, and were first used in 1495 for Cardinal Bembo's *De Aetna*. Claude Garamond (1480-1561) used Bembo as a model, and so it became the frontrunner of standard European type for the following two centuries. Its modern form was designed, following the original, for Monotype in 1929 and is widely in use today.